Ran

Magic Nation

Ran Van
Magic Nation

◆

DIANA WIELER

A GROUNDWOOD BOOK
Douglas & McIntyre
TORONTO / VANCOUVER / BUFFALO

The author gratefully acknowledges the Manitoba Arts Council for financial assistance.

◆

Copyright © 1997 by Diana Wieler
Reprinted 1999

Groundwood Books / Douglas & McIntyre Ltd.
585 Bloor Street West, Toronto, Ontario M6G 1K5

Distributed in the USA by Publishers Group West
1700 Fourth Street, Berkeley, CA 94710

We acknowledge the support of the Canada Council for the Arts and the Ontario Arts Council for our publishing program.

Library of Congress data is available

Canadian Cataloguing in Publication Data

Wieler, Diana J. (Diana Jean)
RanVan magic nation
"A Groundwood book".
ISBN 0-88899-317-X (bound)
ISBN 0-88899-316-1 (pbk.)
I. Title.
PS8595.I53143R3 1997   jC813'.54   C97-931441-0
PZ7.W53Ra 1997

Cover illustration by Ludmilla Temertey
Cover photograph by Ralph Mercer, Tony Stone Images
Design by Michael Solomon
Printed and bound in Canada by Webcom

For Adam, who bravely battles
his own gangster every day

ONE

RHAN was sick. His head throbbed and his throat felt as if he'd swallowed ground glass. It was only September but he'd cranked up the Mazda's heat, trying to fight the sudden tremors that would seize him every 50 K or so. They worried him; he knew he should pull over. But the issue was time now, so he clung to the steering wheel, squinting as he drove into the sunset. He was on his way from Thunder Bay to Calgary and he'd been on the road for fourteen hours. He had the worst cold he'd had in eighteen years.

Make it to Regina, was all he could think. Make it there before the drugstores close.

He should have stopped in Winnipeg when he'd passed through four hours before. But it was only dinnertime then, and he hadn't really felt bad—just a faint ache in his bones, a slight stuffiness. Totally manageable, Rhan had thought. He was one of those people who hardly ever got sick. Colds passed him over with a trace of sniffles. He could beat the flu with a single early night. And he was proud of the fact that he never took medicine. That's what antibodies were for, right?

But this was the Dark Lord of viruses. The sky ahead was orange and pink but Rhan could feel night chasing him, could see it in his rearview mirror.

A clutch of pain, like a sudden squeeze under his ribs, made him catch his breath. Now what? Rhan wondered. Another squeeze, lower and sharper, filled him with a sense of dread. He didn't know much about colds, but he had a feeling he was going to need a bathroom, real soon.

At that moment, his headlights caught a green highway sign in the dusk: Regina 55 KM.

Okay, he told the Universe. So it's a race. He squeezed the accelerator to the floor.

Rhan Van was eighteen years old, and he talked to the Universe a lot. Not just the planets and stars, although that was part of it. To him, the Universe was the whole thing—time, space, matter. It was a system and a place; it was organized and conscious, a force with a hidden agenda that it sometimes thrust in your face. The Universe could get you three red lights in a row—and then show you the traffic accident you'd missed because of them.

His gran called that force God, but to Rhan it was too big an idea for a single entity. It was easier to think of it as a kind of physics that took a personal interest in your life, or a game constructed around you that overlapped into everybody else's game. But how you played it, and whether you could win or not, he didn't know. Some people called that Destiny.

He was flying toward his own now, but he'd been pointed that direction for a long time, held back and waiting, like a slingshot. He and Gran had moved in with her cousin Zoe, who owned a motel called the Trail's End, three years ago. There was something about running a motel, or living in Thunder Bay, that made you plan earnestly for a different future, Rhan thought. Ever since grade ten he'd known he wanted to be a cameraman.

"Not like in a studio," he'd told Gran, "but one of those guys who goes out and films things while they happen. One of those guys who's *there*."

Gran had been wary. It sounded dangerous.

"There's wars and things, you know. People…get hurt."

"They get hurt without wars, too," Rhan said.

"I don't know," Gran said. "It doesn't sound stable. Don't you want something…"

"With a good pension?" Rhan snapped. "Why not? I've only got forty-seven years to go."

"Don't get smart. You know what I mean. Listen, the only thing certain in this world is bills."

"Then I should work at the mill," Rhan said.

"Not while I still have a pulse," Gran said.

There were four paper mills in and around Thunder Bay. The wet, burnt smell hung over the city like a fog. Every family seemed to have someone who worked there. It was steady, even with the layoffs, and it was good money. People cursed the mill, the long hours and the sweaty labor, the unions and the hierarchy, but they didn't leave it. Good Money made years melt into more years and then into a family. Thunder Bay was full of people who would have gone somewhere and done something, if it weren't for the mill.

There were a number of schools that taught what Rhan wanted, but he'd heard that the Southern Alberta Institute of Technology in Calgary was the best. When he received the application package for Cinema, Television, Stage and Radio, his heart sank.

"It says the course only has space for eighty but every year they receive up to six hundred applications, from all over the country," he told Gran. "Six hundred people," he repeated softly. In his mind's eye he could see them all standing there in front of him.

"The only person you gotta worry about is this one," she said, putting her hand on his shoulder.

Rhan read on. "I've got to write an essay, supply a resume...and a demo tape." He looked up. "I've never even done this! How am I supposed to get a demo tape?!"

"Well, couldn't you rent one of those hand-held things that people are always shoving in your face at picnics?"

"A camcorder," Rhan said glumly. "They'll laugh! And anyway, the deadline is in two weeks. How can I have something good enough in two weeks?"

"Listen, if that's what you can do, then do it," Gran said. "The Lord gives points for trying."

Rhan rented the camcorder, and he cornered Gran's cousin Zoe in her room.

"I need some…help," he said. "You got any spells for videotape?"

Zoe didn't laugh. A former member of Wicca, the international order of white witches, she'd once told him that a spell was only an organized wish— but a wish was a powerful thing.

"First of all, is what you want within your abilities?" Zoe had said. "Is it something you could possibly do?"

Rhan shrugged. "Well, maybe. Yeah."

"And do you really want it?"

"More than anything," Rhan said.

"That's your spell," Zoe said.

He'd gone out, mad and disappointed. He could hardly believe they used to burn people at the stake for this kind of thing.

The first day he shot lots of really boring tape. Rhan had lived in Thunder Bay for three years but through the lens he saw the city fresh: the striped smokestacks of the mill; the carnival of stores crammed full for the people who made Good Money; Lake Superior stretching endlessly, gray on gray.

Despair drove him out, day after day, to film nothing. He had to get into SAIT, was all he could think. Into the program and out of here.

The fourth day, there was a snowstorm. It was already April but winter pulled itself back from the brink and dumped twelve centimeters through the night. When Rhan woke up it was still coming down, wet, relentless. He sagged at his bedroom window.

"Don't tell me you're going out," Gran said when she saw him pulling on his jacket.

"Okay, I won't tell you," Rhan said.

"Then for Pete's sake, don't drive," Gran said. "The roads are a mess."

Rhan waded out, thinking about what Zoe had called his spell. More than anything, he told the Universe, over and over.

He was heading toward one of the mills. He'd seen on the news the night before that the mill-wrights' union was preparing to strike and the action didn't seem well supported by the other unions. There had been an interview with the head of the machinists' union, a square-jawed and stubbly man who looked as if his nose had been broken, at least once.

"I have a family," the machinist said. "No one can afford this stupidity year after year. And I'll say that to anyone's face."

Rhan wasn't the only one who expected trouble. Arriving at the mill, he saw that the Thunder Bay Channel 4 news crew was already on the scene, their big blue van taking up most of the narrow street. Rhan watched the small circus set up—two on camera, a sound person, the reporter and a handful of assistants who all fanned out with precision into the strikers marching through the snow.

And then there's me, Rhan thought. The kid

with the Handi-Cam. He felt so stupid, so non-industry that he couldn't bring himself to cross the street and get into their airspace. Use the zoom, he told himself.

When the machinist showed up in an army-green parka, leading a small group, the striking millwrights began to cluster, too. The argument rose up quickly. Even across the street Rhan caught the tail end of angry words. But he wasn't listening, he was concentrating, captivated by the new, abrupt movement in his viewfinder—dark figures against the gray-and-white background. Rhan could feel the excitement running through him in a low hum. The rest of the world didn't seem to exist. The challenge was all here, inside the magic frame.

The shove came suddenly. The man in the green parka staggered back and fell. Rhan took a step to keep him in focus, his heart running. The machinist pulled himself out of the snow calmly but one of his supporters was furious, shouting, swearing; the others had to hold him back. This was heating up.

Then Rhan turned. He didn't think about it. There just seemed to be a call, like a shout to his right. He turned with the tape running, the news crew a blur as his lens sped over them until he focused on their van, sitting silently in the snowy road.

Realization was a pang. There was nothing here. What the hell was he doing? He'd gone off shot and there was nothing here?!

And then the police cruiser slid into his magic frame, moving too fast, wheels turned as it tried to stall the long, icy slide into the rear-end of the Channel 4 news van.

When his clip aired at six o'clock, it was the most thrilling five seconds of his life.

◆

Rhan made it to Regina's Cornwall Centre Mall by 8:45 P.M. He found the washrooms by 8:46. I win, he told the Universe.

There were mirrors over the sinks. Washing his burning face, he realized he didn't look like a man who was winning at anything. He had grown a lot in the last three years, an exhaustive spurt that took him to five-eight and left him thinner than he would have liked. He wasn't gaunt but he didn't scare anybody, either.

Except maybe now, Rhan thought. His glasses didn't hide the hollows under his eyes, and his nose was raw and red from blowing. His long dark hair was past his shoulders and he usually kept it pulled back in a ponytail. Today, though, it was loose, clinging to his neck and forehead with sweat; the chills that had shaken him on the road were a fever now. Everything hurt. He was eighteen but he wanted someone to put him to bed.

Don't be pathetic, Van, he told himself. Get medicated and get on with it.

There was a drugstore in the mall, not far from the food court. It wasn't long until closing but there were still people milling about. Rhan noticed a group of young people, some his age and some older, handing out pamphlets to anyone who'd take one. There was a sameness to them—short haircuts and military boots—that made him think of cadets or missionaries. He ducked around them. He wasn't an army kind of guy.

The drugstore was overwhelming—shelf after shelf of bottles and packages. He had no idea what to buy. An expectorant? That sounded gross. Nasal spray? Not up *my* nose, buddy, Rhan thought. There were pills for sinus pain, syrup for coughs. Where was the stuff for total system breakdown? What did you buy when everything had gone wrong?

And while he was standing there, an antihistimine in one hand and a decongestant in the other, he felt a faint and familiar pull. Barely physical and barely there, it was more like an expectancy or anticipation. The way a pin would feel if a magnet were across the room.

He didn't even look up.

I'm sick, he told the Universe. I'm not ready for anything.

Still the call was growing stronger, more insistent: the sense that he was needed, or he would be.

Rhan was getting mad. A headache thudded against his temples and he could feel the fever pass through him in dizzying waves of heat. Yeah, he was concerned about people, but didn't it matter how he felt? Didn't anybody care about *him*? I'm staying right here, he told the Universe. The answer is No.

Except he had to go to the bathroom again.

Damn! He put the two medicines back and grabbed a third—his best guess. Waiting anxiously in line for the cash register, he noticed a display of children's basketballs on sale. Brightly colored and smaller than normal, each was about the size of a ten-pin bowling ball. On impulse Rhan picked up a purple and black one, and was surprised by how well filled it was. Rock solid, he thought, like the real thing.

"That's a great price," the cashier said as she put the ball in a bag with the medicine. "Summer clearance."

"Yeah," Rhan said. He grabbed his change and ran.

Hurrying through the mall to the washrooms, he couldn't understand what had just happened. He didn't even like basketball, and if he had, he would have bought a regulation-sized ball.

That was stupid, he told himself. You don't have the money to blow on impulse stuff. Take it back.

But when he returned, the drugstore was closed.

He swore out loud. He had the ball in his hand; he felt like firing it at something.

It'd probably just ricochet and hit me in the head, Rhan thought as he pushed wearily through the mall exit.

"My purse!"

The cry came from his right but his eyes caught on the runner who raced past, a blur of denim heading into the parking lot. Horns blared but the young man was fast and agile as he dodged traffic. All around people turned to look. Nobody moved.

And Rhan understood why he was standing there, within range, a projectile in his hand. The sickness in him was suddenly dim, pushed aside by the surge of blue energy he could almost hear rushing through his veins. *Stop the guy. Stop him now!*

For a single second he felt really manipulated. For that second he hesitated.

For God's sake, worry about it later! He dropped his bag and pulled back, lining up the throw. He'd only have one shot at this but he could feel the connections clicking inside him—power and aim and distance. He could do this.

And then the car hit the runner. Rhan saw him go over the hood as if in slow motion, the sickening, powerless slide of a rag doll. The purse spun out, released. The man's body didn't make a sound as it hit the pavement.

Tires screamed, the car stopped. The door flew open and the driver burst out. Older, with thinning gray hair. Somebody's father.

"Oh, my God! I didn't even see...my God!"

People were moving now, some drawing in closer, others hurrying away. The driver was bent over the crumpled young man.

17

"Somebody call 911!" His voice was thick, strangled.

Rhan could see the runner's face against the pavement, long black hair splayed out, his own age. It was then that he realized he was still holding the ball, frozen with it.

"I know what you were going to do."

Rhan turned. He'd seen the young woman in the mall. She was one of the cadets he'd seen earlier, the kids in the army boots.

"It was the right thing," she said. She thrust a pamphlet into his free hand. "You're like us. You're mad and you're not afraid."

Rhan stepped back. He could see the driver leaning against his car, a hand over his face. A woman with a shopping cart was giving the mall's location on her cellular phone. It seemed to take forever before the young man on the ground finally moved, a weak push, as if he was trying to get up.

"Are you all right?" the girl said to Rhan.

He turned and started to walk, fast. Then he was running, then driving. He drove thirty kilometers into the darkness, until the city of Regina wasn't even a glow in his rearview mirror. Then he pulled over onto the paved shoulder of the TransCanada Number One and fired the little basketball into the gigantic prairie night.

TWO

RHAN Van had never believed in Santa Claus. He had almost no memory of his life before kindergarten, but by the time he was five he knew enough about people and the world to realize how unreasonable the whole concept was. Why would a stranger give you presents? What did he want in return? Rhan didn't doubt the magic—flying reindeer were not a problem. It was Santa's motives he couldn't believe. A babysitter once dragged him down to a shopping center for the traditional Christmas photograph. He was in grade one or two—he'd seen the picture—but he remembered the day from the inside, the scratchy turtleneck sweater that became even hotter and scratchier waiting in the awful line.

Finally it was his turn on the red velvet lap. "Smile, smile," the photographer urged, but Rhan was defiant. Hands clenched, teeth gritted inside his closed mouth; it was all they were going to get. The Santa-person looked unnerved but he had a job to do.

"What would you like for Christmas?" he asked.

"To get out of this chair," Rhan said, and they let him.

But he didn't mind getting his picture taken, and there were lots of him at five and six and seven, decked out for play or on his birthday, which fell on the most sacred day of all—Halloween. He could make a costume out of anything; Gran was always on the lookout for her "good" bath towels, which made excellent capes and vanished regularly. When she asked about them, he told her he needed them for the Magic Nation.

"You had it mixed up," Gran told him later with a smile. "You were probably trying to say 'imagination.'"

"Maybe," Rhan said, but he remembered that from the inside, too—the glorious expansion, the sense of being somewhere different but real, of being larger. And in the same way the Santa thing was unreasonable, the Magic Nation made perfect sense. There had to be a place where you could go and everybody was magic, where you could do and be anything. How could you keep getting up in the morning if there wasn't?

He didn't think it was just for him. It didn't matter if you were naughty or nice, or if everybody else had parents and you only had a grandmother. The Magic Nation just *was*, like air. You didn't have to deserve it any more than you had to deserve your shadow.

When he got older, he packed up his costumes in boxes. He didn't talk about the Magic Nation but he didn't have to, because he discovered it was all around him. Comics and books and video games— worlds crowded with champions and crackling with power and sorcery.

"Violent rot," Gran said mildly, when she noticed. But it didn't really trouble her. She thought of it as boy stuff.

It troubled other people. As years went by, Rhan realized that everybody had an opinion—in school, on TV—about what was "worthy" fantasy. Something written by a dead Greek was more noble than a game you lived and played on a screen. It made Rhan mad. Didn't these people have a Magic Nation of their own? Why worry about his?

And yet you couldn't escape the pressure forever. If you wanted peace you had to make that life private, pack it away like costumes or hide it under the bed like comics. It was no accident that most of the games were meant to be played alone. But that wasn't like not believing.

By the time he was eighteen, Rhan had known for three years that he was a knight, an employee of the Universe. Incredible things happened to him sometimes—bursts of strength or speed or agility that ran through him, as brief and exhilarating as lightning, and let him be the one who made the difference. Sometimes it sharpened his intuition, and on rare occasions he even got advance warnings, cryptic previews that were like dreaming while he was awake.

Being a knight, being in that electric moment of helping someone, saving someone, was the most extraordinary thing he knew.

It's all those *other* moments, Rhan thought. The

power was not something he could summon. It didn't earn him money; it didn't get him dates. It just made him feel separate from everyone else on the planet.

In grade twelve he'd taken anthropology. The instructor, Rhan decided, had gone into teaching so he could be certain of having an audience every day. Mr. Monette had a lot of pet theories and one of them was about cultural groups.

"It's not racism," Monette said, over and over. "People naturally congregate and promote others who are like them. They want to be with their own kind. The key to success in society is to find your group."

My kind, Rhan thought, doesn't gather in groups.

He'd only met one other who was like him. Lee Dahl called himself the Iceman, and he'd been obsessed with the same arcade video game as Rhan. Then he'd become obsessed with Rhan. Once they stopped trying to kill each other, triumph over each other, they had nearly been friends, for the five minutes it took the Iceman to leave Thunder Bay. He was swift and he had aim, and they had shared a vision. Rhan didn't know if that made Lee Dahl a knight but he was something, and he knew Rhan was, too.

In the quiet, lonely years that followed, Rhan had gone looking for his own answers. He'd read books; Zoe had a lot of them. Mostly paperbacks from the 1970s—people who claimed to bend spoons with their minds, got telepathic warnings or left their bodies. Some of it was interesting; some of it was outright strange. None of it was him. And in all that he read, nothing ever told him what he needed to know most. Why? What was this power really for? What the hell was the big picture?

He needed that big picture really bad right now. Driving the straight and endless highway, four lanes running through a black hole, there was nothing to distract him. Rhan kept seeing it—the last few seconds as the young man ran, the lilting motion of his black hair against the back of his denim jacket, the sudden wrench of impact, the slide over the hood. Rhan had made mistakes before. He'd screwed up royally, even hurt people by accident or stupidity. But this time he'd failed. The Universe had spoken to him and he'd hesitated.

There were other people in the parking lot, a voice seemed to say inside him. None of them stopped him, either.

But none of them had been maneuvered there to stop him, Rhan argued back. None of them was a knight.

For God's sake, the guy was a thief! He stole somebody's purse.

And he deserved to get hit by a car for that? And the driver—did he deserve to feel like that?

There was nothing here that looked like justice. There was a lot that looked like cruelty, and the worst part was that he wasn't surprised. Rhan had been thinking about cruelty lately, wondering if he and the Universe were really on the same side.

He drove into Calgary at dawn, a dead man. On another day the city might have seemed beautiful, far-flung and orderly, concrete towers against the backdrop of mountains, distant and blue in the early light. But it was all he could do to keep his eyes open.

There were student residences on the SAIT campus, two towers of apartments, but they'd been booked full. Zoe had found him a basement suite within walking distance, a simple place—kitchen, bathroom and a living room with a pull-out couch. The people who lived upstairs were friends of Zoe's.

"Great," Rhan had said. "How many in their coven?"

Zoe smiled. "Just the two."

He had the keys in his pocket and he already knew the way; he'd spent his nights studying maps of Calgary. It was amazing what you could do, Rhan thought, when you didn't have a social life.

Number 105 Dalhousie was a raised bungalow with a cedar front. Two big spruce trees in the front yard hid most of the house, and what was left of the grass was overgrown and wild. Rhan could see one living-room window; there was a dreamcatcher hanging in it, and a gray-and-white cat watching him solemnly from the back of a couch. There were low windows along the ground that probably belonged to his suite.

His whole body was crying out for sleep, but he realized the night wasn't over. The car was packed right full, and he knew exactly what was at the bottom of the trunk, under it all, because he'd loaded it himself.

The sheets, Van. He felt himself sag. As badly as he wanted a bed, he was too tired. He'd sleep on the couch as it was, even the floor if he had to.

There was an entrance at the side of the house. Rhan let himself into a small foyer that doubled as a laundry room. To his right was a short flight of stairs up to a closed door—his landlords, the witches. To the left, beyond the washer and dryer, was his door. When he opened it he stumbled into darkness so complete that for moments he was blind. He groped along six feet of wall for the switch.

When he found the light he saw that he was in his kitchen. Small and spare, it had dark cupboards and avocado appliances—1975, in all its glory. There was a dinette table with a single red-vinyl chair.

He turned away, thoroughly depressed, toward the living room. There in the center of it was the couch, already pulled out and made up with smooth blue sheets, a deep quilt and three pillows. The covers were turned down the way mothers did it on TV.

For a moment Rhan just stood, blinking in disbelief. It seemed like a miracle, a gift. He didn't even know these people. He took off his glasses and set them on the counter. He pulled his shirt over his head and dropped it on the floor. He lost the rest of his clothes walking—runners, jeans, socks, even his underwear in a straight trail, and slid stark naked into the clean sheets that wrapped around him in a whispering caress.

He slept for thirteen hours.

THREE

WELCOME CTSR 1ST YEAR! THIS PARTY IS THE FIRST PARTY OF THE REST OF YOUR LIFE. WALLOW IN THE MUD OF HUMANITY—LEARN TO RECOGNIZE YOUR OWN KIND. ONE WILD NIGHT ONLY, BROUGHT TO YOU BY CTSR 2ND YEAR. "WE DO NOT EAT OUR YOUNG."

SATURDAY NIGHT, 8TH FLOOR, BLDG. A., RES.

Rhan read the sign twice. It was taped to the door of H Building, home of Cinema, Television, Stage and Radio, on the SAIT Campus. Classes didn't start until Monday but he'd come to the sprawling campus to look around, to try all the doors.

Rhan wasn't well but he was better; sleep and a shower had beaten the virus a few steps back. He was smoking his first cigarette since the Manitoba/Saskatchewan border, feeling lightheaded and excited in the cool Calgary night.

He wanted to go to this party.

But he didn't move. He finished the cigarette and still he stood there, hesitating. Before this summer he'd trusted people a lot more. Now he couldn't fight the small, irrational fear that he was being set up.

For Pete's sake, they don't even know you, he told himself. Get a grip, Van! You'll never get through this course if you can't even be with people. He started determinedly toward the twin towers of student residence.

He had imagined SAIT a hundred times, but it was still hard to believe he was really here. Some of the buildings were old stone but most were modern, connected by lighted walkways and generous lawns. Traffic hummed, distant and dim, beyond the edge of the campus, but the trees seemed to catch the sound and rustle it away in their leaves. The air was clean; he kept expecting the next breeze to bring the odor of wet, burnt paper—the smell of the mill, the smell of money—and it didn't happen. It wasn't such a bad thing to be far from home.

The note had only said the party was on the eighth floor, and riding up in the elevator, Rhan wondered how he would know which suite. There were two other guys in the cubicle but by the time he thought of asking them, he was at his floor.

When the elevator door opened, the blast of music and people hit him full in the face. If this party had started in an apartment, it had outgrown it in a serious way.

For a moment Rhan stood, feeling like he'd just left his spaceship. This was supposed to be for First Years but everyone seemed to know each other, really well. Hands clasped shoulders, arms circled waists. Maybe he should get back in the elevator.

Suddenly a young man in the crowd whirled on them. There was a brightness to him, or maybe it was his hair—blond running to red. He had the kind of face that should have had freckles, but didn't. He pointed at the guy next to Rhan.

"Engineering!" he cried. He pointed to the next one. "Engineering!"

He waggled a finger at Rhan, grinning. "But that one, with the lean and hungry look, the unkempt, the tired, the shunned—that's one of ours."

There was a lilt to his voice, a singsong accent that Rhan couldn't quite place. The two guys shouldered through the crowd. "Frigging media."

The copper-haired young man turned and called out after them. "You can always tell an engineer. He's the one walkin' tall, a survey pole up the arse!"

Rhan caught his breath. In Thunder Bay, that was considered an "opening." As in, "I wanted to belt him and he gave me an opening." To his astonishment, the engineering students lumbered on around the corner.

The man with the accent turned back to Rhan. "I'm right, aren't I, lad? CTSR—first year?" Rhan nodded. The other threw his arms skyward.

"I have the gift! Touched by the hand of the Lord!"

Benevolent laughter, all down the hall.

He grabbed Rhan's hand and started shaking it. "Devon McGuinness—lately of Calgary but born in the center of civilization, County Cork, Ireland."

Rhan was grinning. "Rhan Van. Lately of Thunder Bay, but I got out alive."

Devon laughed. "Well, then, we've saved anoth-

29

er soul. Celebrate your redemption. Around that corner you'll find an apartment, and sitting on the kitchen counter is a beautiful lady named Shona, guarding the booze. You tell her Devon McGuinness bought you a beer."

It was slow going. The hallway was crowded, and people kept grabbing his hand and shaking it. "I'm Lynn Neville." "I'm Amin Habib." Rhan had never been around people who called themselves by two names. As if they were campaigning, he thought. As if they wanted you to remember them.

Most were hard to forget. There was that brightness again that he couldn't quite place. Either eccentric—jackets with beer tabs stapled into designs—or the clean-cut scrubbed look of expensive haircuts. He quickly learned that was the Second Year On-Air look; students poised for a job at any moment. Some of the students were his age, but he was surprised by how many were older, maybe in their twenties. He heard a woman talking about her kids. He hadn't expected this. He'd come to SAIT expecting to be in *school*, and he wasn't.

He'd never seen people touch each other like this. Men, women—there seemed to be no divisions, just one great flowing embrace as everyone squeezed around each other, grabbed shoulders, even hugged. Rhan was uneasy in the crowd and more than once he pulled away suddenly, his heart running. He didn't like to be grabbed.

He made it to the kitchen and Shona was sitting

on the counter just like Devon had said. Rhan gave her the message and she shook her head.

"That's seventeen he's bought tonight. More heart than brains, I think." She handed him a beer anyway, grinning. "It's a good thing I love him for his body."

There was a commotion, voices calling over the music.

"Shh, shh! This is it! Let's go."

Go where? Rhan wondered, but someone tugged his arm, pulling him into a circle that was forming fast in the tiny living room. There were two, actually, one within another, made by linking arms. Rhan realized he was linked to a girl on his right side, a guy on his left.

He broke the hold, alarmed. The guy laughed. "You First Years! It's not a date or anything. Everybody does Circle."

There was nowhere to go; he was caught in this. Then he noticed that the whole room was swaying and he was swaying with it. And everyone who knew the words was singing—singing!—along with the song that blared out of the stereo. Rhan started listening and he forgot to be mortified.

We are the ones
Points of light
We blazed the trail
Burning all night
Look into the camera, baby

Speak into the mike
You think you're building you
But we are the ones
Writing your life.
Better watch how you live
Better watch where you sleep
The face you show to us
Is the one you get to keep.
And if our gaze should burn you
Keep you awake at night
Remember that you asked for love
From the points of light.

The song ended and the whole room broke apart and burst into applause. Rhan clapped along numbly, feeling a little overloaded by the experience. The touching, the singing—and that song, he thought. What did it mean? He didn't know if he liked this or not. But it seemed to him there was something, a feeling, a buzz, that hadn't been in the room before.

"Well, that was the stupidest goddamn thing I've ever been through." The young man who had moved in next to him had a square jaw and too much forehead. Above that his dark-brown hair seemed to go straight up in a wiry wall, like a helmet.

"I came here to meet people, not hold hands and sing. Like, what is this—camp?"

He said it with a trace of a sneer, like a bad

stand-up comic. In that instant, Rhan decided that he *liked* Circle, if only because this jerk didn't.

The young man stuck out his hand, a poor imitation of a Second Year. "Robert Arnott, but you can call me Bob."

"Okay," Rhan said. Please, he told the Universe. Let him be a radio major, or film. He didn't offer his name and Bob didn't ask.

"So, what's your major?"

"TV—Production," Rhan said.

"Tech junkie, eh?" Bob grinned. "Well, that's what we used to call them at Cable, where I did my pre-training. Hey, no offense, though. I did it, too. Camera one, camera two. Hauled cables, did set-up. All the shit work."

Now, though, Bob was beyond that. He was majoring in Television—Writing and Producing. "But we'll be in first term together. They want me to do Studio anyway."

Rhan was looking around desperately for somebody else to talk to. Devon McGuinness had come into the kitchen again and was leaning against the counter, one arm draped over Shona's dangling legs. But his lips were engaged.

"So, where'd you take your pre-training?" Bob asked.

Rhan was saved by a hush. It started at the door and seemed to move through the suite like a wave. It didn't silence the room, but it softened it. Bob looked. Everyone looked.

The young woman was small and beautiful, even in jeans and a T-shirt. Her short brown hair seemed to be streaked and dusted in gold, and she wore a coral-colored sweater tied around her waist. Somehow she managed to look cool in the overheated apartment. Rhan watched her as she wandered from person to person, brief greetings and a smile, sometimes laughter. He guessed she was in her mid-twenties, a Second Year for sure. She had their poise, or beyond that, he thought. This one was a point of light.

"We're graced," Devon said quietly behind Rhan, but there was no malice in his voice. "The *Wunderkind* favors us with her presence."

The wonder child, Rhan thought. "Second Year?" he asked, turning back to Devon.

The Irishman was dumbfounded. "What god-forsaken rock did you say you came from, man? That's Marlene Foye, as in the national show, The Foye Report? That's in addition to Channel 9 News at 6 and …"

Devon broke off suddenly. Rhan realized the hush had come to them, surrounded them. He turned.

Marlene Foye had stopped in front of him, a breath of perfume and gold dust. Her eyes danced over him briefly, up and down. She did not hold out her hand.

"Rhan Van." She smiled faintly. "I'm so glad you made the second cut, but I was sure you would. Your tape was…interesting." She turned to go, glancing back over her shoulder at him. "See you next semester."

She didn't linger but headed directly for the door out. The crowded room seemed to melt out of her way.

"She also teaches here," Devon said, but he was looking him up and down, the way Marlene Foye had.

"Just who the hell are you?" Bob demanded.

Rhan wanted to snap something back—that he was the tech junkie who hadn't taken *any* pre-training—but the hot, crowded room seemed to press in on him suddenly. He felt a wave of nausea sweep over him, the virus rearing up for a violent last stand. He needed air, right now.

He squeezed his way through the group and this time it was worse, every jostle, every nudge of a stranger accelerating the alarm that had come out of nowhere. He felt surrounded, a lash of memory and panic. People were looking now but it didn't matter. He had to get out.

He broke into the hallway, where the crush wasn't as bad. Down a corridor he saw the glowing red Exit sign for the stairwell. Thank God.

A hand seized his shoulder. Rhan spun around, his right arm up to ward off the blow. The young woman cried out, startled, and stumbled back. Her drink glass hit the wall but didn't break.

The crowd behind them hushed. For an instant Rhan and the girl just stared at each other. She had tawny skin and shiny black hair, straight and long, dark eyes over high cheekbones. Her white blouse was stained in a spray across the front, from the drink.

"I was going to ask if you were all right," she said. "I guess you're not."

"I'm sorry," Rhan blurted. He bolted for the stairs. Eight flights—sixteen sets of two—a long zigzag downward, the motion shaking him like a soft drink. He hit the main level and burst out the door, just in time.

The stairwell opened out onto a dark, secluded side of the building and Rhan was grateful, once he could be grateful for anything, which wasn't for a while. Finally he leaned against the cement block wall, gasping in the cool night. He knew he should crawl back upstairs, apologize all around and maybe try to sop up some of the beer out of the carpet. He didn't think he had the fortitude, or the nerve.

Great exit, Van, he told himself. Grand finale. You're such a screw-up.

There was the sudden scrape of metal as the door opened. Devon stepped out, holding it open behind him. Embarrassed, Rhan froze along the wall, but it did no good.

"Are you all right, then?" Devon asked.

"Yeah, sort of," Rhan managed sheepishly. "I've got the flu." He took a step away from the mess, his face burning. "Look, I spilled a drink upstairs…"

Devon waved the apology away. "No matter. The

whole shaggin' carpet's the color of beer."

"There's this girl…"

Devon grinned. "She's the one who sent me, wanted to make sure you were all right. Come on, I'll give you a ride home."

Rhan argued that it was only a few blocks and he could make it, but the man wouldn't hear of it. Rhan finally had to point out that Devon could barely stand, let alone drive. The Irishman leaned against the wall in revelation.

"Not only that, I don't think I own a car," he said. Rhan was surprised to hear himself laugh.

When he finally started for home, he felt better with every step. The night seemed filled with wonder. He'd never had this, never seen it—strangers who shook your hand like they were glad to meet you, linked arms with you and sang out loud. He thought of Marlene Foye being sure he would make the second cut; he thought of the girl who'd sent Devon after him. So this was CTSR. He didn't think they were his kind, but he might be willing to be theirs.

FOUR

THE hardest part about being an adult, Rhan thought, was going to bed and getting up again. He'd always been a nighthawk, engines still revving at eleven and midnight and one. As a kid, every evening had been a constant negotiation with Gran for one more show, one more game, one more precious half hour. By high school he was setting his own hours, and the negotiation was all done in the morning.

"Come on, already! You're going to miss the bus."

"I'm getting a ride." *Maybe. If he phoned his friend J.R. within the next two minutes.*

"You've had three late slips already, mister."

"I have not." *It was more like six.*

"I'm not calling you again!"

Except she would, and he knew it. And the whole trick was to pinpoint the exact moment she'd stop calling and come charging up the stairs, and somehow make the impossible two-second leap out of bed and into his clothes so that he could look into her chagrined face and say, "I told you—I'm up."

This summer he'd had a job, and nobody woke him. It was a shock that the last glorious, luxurious few minutes in bed had to be paid for with a panicked dash—no time for breakfast, no time for a shower—and at the end of it there was no late slip.

There was a foreman with disgust in his eyes and hell in his heart, waiting to give you the shit jobs that everybody else had passed up.

That's when Rhan became a two-alarm man. He had an electronic clock/radio but it had a snooze bar, allowing him to slip again and again into those wonderful, timeless pockets of sleep. It never came charging up the stairs. Finally one night he got an old alarm clock, basic machinery in baby blue plastic that actually had to be wound up, that ticked so loudly he could hear it with the door shut. He put it in the bathtub.

The next morning there was a fire—he knew because he heard the bells, clanging madly in an empty, metallic firehall. The sound lifted him two feet off the bed and vaulted him into the bathroom, where he seized the offensive thing and pounded it into silence. When Zoe hurried in, he was sitting on the side of the tub, heart still pounding, his head leaning against the wall tile.

"What is that godawful noise?!"

"The rest of my life," Rhan said numbly.

It was a barbaric system, but it worked, and that was the thing about being an adult: you had to do what worked. The first morning of classes in Calgary, Rhan found himself standing in his empty shower stall at 6 A.M., holding the baby blue monster with both hands.

"If you had a throat I would choke you," he told it.

But once he was in the shower, the warm water worked its usual magic and he was excited and glad to be in the day. His life was starting, and he needed only one more miracle to get him there. In half an hour he was clean and dry and dressed, his hair tied back neatly, the binder that was his class module tucked under his arm, ready for his reward.

"Coffee," Rhan told the convenience store clerk, snapping the money onto the counter.

Coffee had become important. He'd always liked the smell of it, how it filled up the kitchen and meant that people were home. But he didn't drink it himself until this summer and then only at night—he didn't have the co-ordination to perk anything at sunrise.

At first he drank it black, suffering through the taste because it seemed more grown up. Then he began experimenting with cream and sugar, just a dash of each, and created something that was really quite tolerable, even enjoyable. And there was no denying the kick of it, subtle and sensual, warmth in his throat, caffeine buzzing through him like encouragement.

And then one rushed and bleary morning he stopped by a convenience store on the way to the mill and bought one to go, and standing in the cool morning air he had coffee and his first cigarette of the day together and it was *love*. He was fully wired by the time he hit Dominion Paper. He did it every morning after that.

Your problem, Rhan told himself, is that you have an addictive personality. But he was amazed that a need he didn't even know he had could be so fierce once awakened. And he was amazed that the secret to the adult world was so simple: barbarism and chemicals.

Rhan walked out of the convenience store with both hands full, balancing all his equipment, looking for a place to set everything down so he could light up. There were no benches outside the store, so he rounded the corner that gave way to a little row of renovated houses that were now stores. There had to be a fence or something, he thought.

The store window seemed to hit him in the chest. It was the size of the whole wall, like a glass showcase set into somebody's house. The painted sign said *The Odyssey* but a single glance told him it wasn't about one journey into the Magic Nation, it was about all of them. A poster of X-Men's Wolverine dominated one whole end of it, his bulging muscles and comic-brilliant colors—yellow and blue and black—snarling at the world. Life-sized and vivid next to the faded clapboard of the house, Wolverine looked more real than real. Also part of the display was a hammer—not the kind you used for nails, but an old hammer, broad and square, the kind a Norse god would choose.

Rhan could see beyond the glass—comics and role games, figurines and paraphernalia crowding the shelves and walls. From Star Wars to King

Arthur, all the heroes were there, brought together in a glorious swirl of colors and darkness.

For a moment Rhan just stood there, his heart in his throat. The store wasn't open and he was glad. Not that it mattered—that part of his life was over and gone. But he was just…glad.

He set his module and coffee on top of a mail box while he lit his cigarette, then started toward the campus.

"I need a job," he told the Universe, as if the Universe didn't know.

◆

Studio A was a large room with a high ceiling and a cool metallic smell to the air. Rows of black metal lights were suspended from tracks, varying in size from a tin can to a deep kitchen wok. Against the far wall there was a small set: a raised platform with two cheap office chairs angled in toward each other, a painted cityscape behind them. Under the regular fluorescent lights it all looked astonishingly cheap, a cardboard kind of reality that wouldn't fool anybody.

Metal folding chairs were set up but Rhan was wandering, examining the room along with the other twenty students. He recognized a few faces from the party, and they smiled back as they recognized him. Some people were chatting but no one was hugging. Without the beer, without the bolstering presence of Second Years, shyness hung on all of them like too-big clothes.

Across the room, he saw Bob Arnott, and decided he would pretend he didn't. You could have a group, Rhan thought, but that didn't mean you had to like everybody in it. Today Bob was wearing a sweater and white shirt and a brilliant cranberry-colored tie. The knot beamed out at his throat like a laser.

Rhan owned one tie. It had Popeye on it.

People were sitting down now and Rhan could finally get close to the cameras. They drew him in like magnets. Two were angled in toward the set, and a third backed against the wall. Each was a top-heavy metal box on a pedestal, with a small screen that was shaded by a hood. There was a lever for tilting, Rhan guessed, and a metal circle joined by spokes to the pedestal. The whole thing was taller than he was. He wondered if it was heavy to move around.

Before he could touch it, a hand caught his arm. Brown eyes were drilling into his.

"Please don't touch the equipment," the instructor said. "This piece of metal cost more than my house." He seemed to realize he had a grip on Rhan's arm, and let it go.

Rhan slunk over toward the chairs and quickly found a place for himself. So that was Lesson One, Van, he told himself. Try not to have any more today.

There was a solid bang as the door was shut. The remaining students dropped into their seats and the instructor centered himself in front of them. Tall and thin, there was a sharpness to him that was visible through his clothes, a tweed blazer over jeans and a T-shirt. His long brown hair was pulled back in a ponytail but it was his mustache that caught the eye. Not quite the handlebar version, it was luxurious and thick, nearly covering his upper lip. To Rhan, who only had to shave every second day, it was a great mustache.

"Okay, let's get going. I'm your first-term studio instructor, Mark Boutiniere. People call me a lot of things and I probably earn all of them." A small ripple of laughter. "But you can call me Mark. For sixty-eight hours this term this studio is your world, and I am its god. So let's start off with the commandments."

He looked at Rhan. "Thou shalt not touch equipment thou hast not been prepped to touch."

Open laughter. Rhan grinned sheepishly. The studio god barely smiled.

"Everything in here is horrifically expensive and we don't have the funding for stupid mistakes," Mark said. "There are *lightbulbs* that are sixty bucks each…"

The door rattled just then, somebody trying to get in. Mark strode over, but before he even touched the knob, he turned back to his audience.

"A hundred dollars says it's a woman." He swung the door open.

"Thank you," Mark told the astonished girl.

The room burst into laughter and applause, but Rhan did not clap. Her dark hair was pulled up in a high ponytail and gleamed, wet. She seemed to have run to class straight from the shower. She wore a baggy sweatshirt and tight leggings, but he would have known her in a burlap bag. The Saturday Night girl.

"The second commandment: Thou shalt not be late." Mark closed the door decisively. "This class starts at 8 A.M. At 8:02 I shut that door and it's locked. If you don't make it, that's an F for the day."

The room was very still. Rhan felt the news settle inside him. He was a two-alarm man but that didn't mean he never had relapses. He didn't want an F on any day.

The girl grinned, embarrassed. She started toward the chairs, but the instructor stopped her with a hand on her shoulder.

"The assignment, please," Mark said.

Her smile faded. She didn't know what he was talking about. Neither did Rhan.

"The lighting assignment that was on the third page of your Television Production Module," the instructor said, his voice rising to include them all. "The simple, five-minute assignment that you would have seen if you'd even opened the module that was mailed to you over two weeks ago."

Rhan had the module with him, the binder filled with pages of typed notes, diagrams and assignments. When it had arrived, he'd glanced through it

45

excitedly, but he hadn't actually read it. He'd been too busy getting ready to come here, and anyway, wasn't that what the classes were for?

The girl had the module, too, clutched in one arm as she shifted uncomfortably in front of her staring audience. She looked anxious, cornered. Rhan was getting mad. Why didn't Mark let her sit down already?

"I put in that assignment every year," Mark was saying, "and you know why? Because that one page pretty much tells me who's going to do well in this studio and who's not. It tells me who gives a damn about being here..."

"That's not fair," Rhan blurted. Heads turned, including Mark's. Rhan felt the heat in his face but he had to keep going—he'd started this.

"You can't judge somebody because of one day, one assignment. I mean, if it was hidden..."

"Did *anyone* see this assignment?" The instructor's voice rolled out on top of his. "Did anyone do it?"

Fourteen hands went up, fourteen out of twenty. Bob Arnott waved the sheet in his hand like a flag. Mark gestured to the girl to sit down at last, and put his fists on his hips.

"School's out, boys and girls," he said. "This is real life. You show up for work unprepared, and you let everybody down. Maybe you stop the whole process. The people who hired you lose money. Believe me, they're not going to lose money on you twice. An excuse is no excuse. It's your job to find out what has to be done."

He let the words soak in. "The fourth commandment: You show up prepared or you don't work. That's an F for the day. If you're working in teams, everybody's ready or everybody gets an F."

There was a low murmur of horror and disbelief. Mark's voice softened. "No stars in a studio, people, and no lone gunmen, either. You depend on each other so you have to take care of each other. If somebody's not pulling his weight, you hand him to me. I won't let one person bring you down."

Rhan was ashamed. The hidden assignment still seemed unfair, but Mark's argument was reasonable. What if people had been depending on him today? He had no experience with teams; he'd always been that lone gunman. He decided then that no one was going to get an F because of him.

Mark suddenly clapped his hands together. "Let's get to work. Everybody who did the assignment will take turns lighting the set. Single subject. Everybody else, sit against the wall and do the sheet. You can join us when you're done."

There was a scraping and banging as the students cleared the folding chairs. Rhan saw the Saturday Night girl heading for the wall. Mark was right—school was out. He walked over to her, determined.

"I owe you an apology," Rhan said.

The young woman got quickly to her feet.

"Actually, you owe me a shirt."

"Okay," Rhan said. He reached for his wallet, wondering if he had enough, but she stopped him.

"I mean, not right now. Later—I'll tell you when." She grinned wickedly. "Don't worry, you'll pay."

Rhan couldn't help but smile back. He liked standing this close. She smelled clean, a fresh floral scent that was probably her shampoo. With her hair pulled up, he saw a fine gold chain around her neck. There seemed to be a pendant hanging from it, but it was next to her skin, under her sweatshirt. He wondered what it was.

"I'm glad you're feeling better," she said. "But why'd you take a swing at me?"

Rhan felt a pull of caution. "Claustrophobia?"

The girl cocked her head, studying him. "Not bad. I give you four out of ten—full marks for originality."

She knew he was lying, and not that well. "We'd better do that assignment," she said, settling against the wall.

Rhan opened his module. All he had to do was read the Introduction to Lighting and fill in the word definition blanks. But it was hard to keep his mind on the task. He didn't know if the apology had worked or not.

"I'm Jen," she whispered suddenly, without looking at him. "You owe me a drink, too."

Rhan soared through the page.

Magic was happening in the studio. Student after student sat on the cardboard set to be lit—spotlight, backlight and fill. It looked all right from where Rhan stood but when Mark went to the control room—a small darkened cavern joined to the studio by a narrow window—he switched on the cameras. On the studio monitor the scene leapt out in brilliant color: the cheap backdrop looked solid and professional; the girl in the chair seemed to glow with health. Rhan could barely believe it. This was done with *light*?

Mark kept moving the chairs so that the lights had to be repositioned. Rhan waited for his turn, watching the process intently. After missing the sheet, he didn't want to screw this up, too. Suddenly he was engulfed in a wave of aftershave.

"I could have told you—a good demo tape won't save you in the studio," Bob Arnott said. "Any idiot can point a camera."

"And I bet you're the guy who proved it," Rhan said. Bob stepped away; he seemed to be grappling for a comeback. But just then it was Rhan's turn.

"Give it your best shot," Bob said, gesturing expansively toward the set.

Rhan was mad, and he could feel Mark watching him. Be good, Van, he told himself. You don't have to be fast. He seemed to struggle with the backlight forever; the guy in the chair started to sweat from the heat. When he was finally done, Rhan looked over to where Mark was leaning against the wall, arms crossed over his chest.

"Yeah," the instructor nodded finally. "That's okay."

"I'm fried," the guy said, pushing out of the chair.

"Don't be a baby. He made you look great," Mark said. Rhan felt the hope leap inside him. He looked for Bob, but Mr. Studio had disappeared.

The class was over too soon. Two hours had somehow evaporated. As the students began to troop out, Jen and the four others dropped their late assignments onto a chair. Rhan thought about following her out, but he held onto his own sheet and waited.

The overhead lights were already off and as Mark flipped switches at the main panel, the whole room fell dim and silent. Rhan watched Mark reposition the cameras easily, deftly—a professional who knew the equipment, even in the dark.

Mark was surprised when he finally turned around.

"Yeah?" he said.

"I wanted to hand this in," Rhan said, holding out the sheet.

"Okay. Just put it there." Mark gestured at the pile on the chair and turned away, heading for his briefcase, which was leaning against the wall. Rhan felt dismissed, but he wasn't ready to go.

"It won't happen again," he called.

"Sure it will." Mark bent down for the case.

"Maybe not this week, or next week, but it will."

Rhan was stung into silence. Teachers weren't supposed to say things like that, were they?

"Don't take it personally, Rhan," Mark said, sauntering back. "You're just…young. No pre-training, no work experience, no study skills. We get a couple like you every year. I burn them out by Christmas. Sometimes they try again a few years later, when they're really ready to be here."

Rhan's face was on fire. "I'm ready to be here," he said. "I earned this. You people chose me…"

"I didn't choose you. Most of us on the panel didn't. Somebody…" Mark hesitated and took a step back. "Look, I'm sorry. Forget it. Do your best."

"I made the cut, I deserve to be here!" Rhan insisted. "I'm going to make it." A beat. "Somebody *what*?"

Mark stood, briefcase in hand, his face grimly set.

Rhan spun around and out. In the hallway he passed Jen and felt a dim pulse of horror. What had she heard? But he didn't stop moving, hurrying through the labyrinth to the crowded main level. There was an elevator but he didn't wait for it. Second level, Communications office. A woman was just pulling on her coat.

"Please…I…need to speak to Marlene Foye." He was surprised to be out of breath. He didn't realize he'd been running.

"I'm afraid she's gone."

"What about after lunch?"

The woman smiled. "Around the end of October, sure. She's really gone—across Canada. I think it's research for her show." She bent down to check a large planner on the desk. "Tory Samuels is covering her classes. Could he help you?"

Rhan shook his head numbly and began backing away, embarrassed by his spell of panic. He was an adult. He had to remember that. He was on his own now.

FIVE

HE'D grown up in a single day. The end of the previous June had been hot, muggy and suffocating in Thunder Bay. Graduation had come and gone. He'd gotten his piece of paper but he didn't go to the ceremony, or the dance. He and Zoe went to the hospital every day.

He'd been introduced to the inside of the hospital when he was sixteen and Gran had been diagnosed with lymphomas. Every visit was only a visit then, as she went through round after round of treatment. They never said "cancer" in their house; it was always "the Big C." Like a gangster, Rhan thought. And everyone was cheerful and toughtalking. They could beat this guy.

For a while it looked like it. But the Big C was a terrible gangster, one who pretended your debt was paid, only to reappear somewhere else later, grinning and monstrous, to tell you how very, very late you were. Two years after the lymphomas had been declared clear, Gran had been diagnosed with acute myelogenous leukemia, and the cancer had quickly gone from the blood to the bone marrow. Rhan could almost imagine the Big C hanging back in the shadows with a smirk, eating their hope like breakfast. Neither Rhan nor Zoe was a potential bone marrow donor.

You couldn't sit very long in somebody's room, looking at them. Hospital beds made people too small, like the soaring ceilings in churches, Rhan thought. But there was hardly anywhere else to go—a cafeteria, a chapel, a smoking room. Sometimes he just walked the hallways, frustrated as hell. It seemed to him that the doctors and staff weren't taking this seriously enough, not treating it like the emergency it was.

"Why aren't they doing something?" he demanded of Zoe.

"Morphine," she told him. "That's what they can do."

It shook him because he knew it was one of the big guns, something they held back until it was too late to become addicted to anything. He walked the hallways more quietly after that.

The good thing about drugs was that they were a wall to pain. He would have gone crazy if he thought she hurt. The bad thing was that they were a wall to you, too, Rhan thought. He could sit and watch the slight rise and fall of her chest as she breathed, but that wasn't like being with someone. He wasn't even sure it was really her. His gran was a big woman, tall and willful. There wasn't a man she couldn't stare down, including him and including Jack Van, the drunk of a husband she'd thrown out long before Rhan was even born.

"And I mean physically," Zoe said. "One hand on his collar, the other on the back of his coat—into the street and his suitcase after him."

The story made Rhan smile because he believed

it. It was this crumpled little person in the big white bed—one hand clutching a tissue in unconscious sleep, a tube in her arm and another up her nose—that he couldn't believe.

On July 10th he had a dream that his car was in Moe's garage. It had been making a noise, a terrible thumping that he knew was something really awful and probably expensive. But when he hurried into the repair bay, the Mazda was sitting where he'd left it, not even up on a hoist.

Moe was calmly wiping his hands on a rag.

"Did you have a look?" Rhan said.

"There's nothing wrong with her," Moe said. "I didn't have to look."

Rhan was furious. The noise was real—he'd heard it. The fury gushed up through his chest and suddenly he was swearing at Moe, curse words he didn't even know that he knew. In the pit of his stomach he felt a cold knot of horror—he'd never yell at this man. But this was his *car*, for Christ's sake, and Moe was supposed to fix the goddamn thing and he wouldn't even goddamn look at it?!

Moe didn't flinch, just kept walking quietly toward him, the abuse rolling off him like water. Rhan was almost choking on rage and panic; he couldn't spew it out fast enough. But when Moe put a hand on his shoulder, the touch silenced him.

"There's nothing wrong with her," Moe said carefully, so he would understand. "She's all right now."

Rhan awoke to the ringing phone.

The funeral was the first day he tied his hair back in a ponytail. It was the first time he noticed it was long enough, the first time it mattered to him to look neat. He was in a rented gray suit and tie—the shirt was his own—and his face surprised him, the squared jaw and cheekbones he hadn't noticed before. When had this happened? It made him uneasy. He didn't know if he was ready to be that man.

Even Zoe noticed. She looked once, then twice. "What a funny time to discover you're handsome," she said with a wan smile.

The other funeral in his life he'd been kept back from; he'd been too small when his mother died and there was too much horror hanging in the air, lingering in people's faces. No one kept him back from this. They seemed to push him up close—front pew and graveside, marching him through the ritual because he was eighteen and a man, pressing the truth into his skin.

It was a small crowd—him and Zoe, Moe Gervais and his family, a few acquaintances he didn't know, a scattering of friends. The only part of the service Rhan remembered hearing was the 23rd Psalm, and then only when the whole group answered back: *The Lord is my shepherd, I shall not want.* He remembered because he wouldn't open his mouth to speak that lie.

Only Moe came back to the Trail's End afterward. The three of them were in the kitchen smoking because there was no reason not to smoke in the house now. He and Moe were sitting at the table; Zoe leaned against the counter. He'd been in a daze since the phone call from the hospital, someone in transit, not thinking about his destination, just swept along by the unstoppable flow of events. Now he'd been plunked down in his life again and he wasn't sure if he was the same person. His plans hadn't changed: he was still going to SAIT and to his surprise, Gran's small insurance policy would cover his two years there, if he worked summers. But school was only school. It didn't tell him where he was supposed to fit in the world. It didn't tell him who he was supposed to be.

"I need a job," he blurted.

"You don't have to worry," Zoe said, her voice tight. "I told you before…"

Moe lifted his hand to silence her. "You'll find it," he said to Rhan. "Everybody has a place."

That night he burned everything. There was a metal barrel out behind the motel cabins, near the shed and within sight of the kitchen window. He could feel Zoe watching him, squinting at him through the blackness, and he didn't care. She was a woman and she wouldn't understand.

His arms were full—all the comics, all the trading cards, all the little toy heroes and their plastic capes. He'd thrown away a lot when he'd left Vancouver but this was the end of it. Some things he hadn't even looked at in years; they'd just been tucked away safe in drawers. But there were no more safe drawers.

He started the fire first and fed his treasure in piece by methodical piece—Superman and Batman and Spiderman and Spawn curling into flame, eaten alive. The one thing that stopped him was a white piece of paper he found stuck between two comics, just a white piece of paper folded into four. He didn't open it; he knew it was the drawing of Arachnaman, the eight-armed superhero he and his friend Darryl had created a hundred years ago. Darryl had done the drawings but Rhan was always the voice—dialogue and story and thought balloons—because he knew Arachnaman from the inside.

It took a long time but he finally let go, and the folded sheet fluttered into the brilliant orange bonfire caught in the rusted drum. Grimly Rhan stood watch as the Magic Nation raged and burned, as it lit up the darkness one last time.

"I need a *job*," he whispered to the Universe.

◆

On a Calgary highway, Rhan was flying. After the morning in Studio A he'd hung on through his afternoon classes, holding himself together until he could make it to his car and cut the emotion loose. Now deep bass guitar vibrated the metal of the car, through the seats and into his bones. What the Mazda's sound system lacked in refinement it made up for in volume. Rhan was totally submerged in it, like swimming underwater. He could see the world beyond his windshield but that didn't mean it was real.

Okay. I've seen worse. You don't scare me.

Calgary's rush hour was its own dimension. It was a city obsessed with moving forward and Rhan was running with it, relishing the snap decisions and split-second turns. He changed lanes on a whim, dove for the gaps, cut people off. This was war and he could do it. His hand never left the shift as he tromped between the gas, the brake and the clutch, burning the day away through all four gears.

I wanted something, is that it? I'm not allowed to want anything, have anything?

He didn't know why this blow was so bad, why the opinion of one man could leave him feeling worthless. You don't even know that it's the truth, Rhan thought. Just because he said it doesn't make it true. And even if it is, you've lived through worse.

But that was the problem. He had lived through a lot. Heartbreak after heartbreak, blow after blow, and somehow he'd kept getting back up, kept trying to hope, to believe in something and do right, while the bully stood over him, waiting.

He was mad at Mark but madder at where it came from. A Universe that gave him the power to help people, but wouldn't let him save himself. A Universe that punished him—punished others—for a second's hesitation. A Universe that let him get close to something he wanted, let him believe he could have it, only to snatch it away and laugh in his face.

You don't scare me. You want to play? Come on.

Sarcee Trail to Richmond Road to Crowchild, highway after highway hooked together and strung out. Rhan was flying, unwinding, swimming in violent sound.

He cut someone off, a dark blue Lexus—executive's car. In seconds he realized he'd picked on the wrong car. It zoomed up to his bumper, dangerously close. He could see the driver's grim, furious face in his rearview mirror. Rhan changed lanes; the Lexus followed, swinging in behind him. He felt the sudden shock of contact, a nudge from behind. Adrenaline shot through his veins, but there was nowhere to go. He was already riding the bumper of the oblivious car in front. Then he saw the sign—an exit just ahead, to the right. But there were two lanes of fairly steady traffic between him and the turn off. Did he risk it?

Another nudge. Shit!

Rhan didn't signal. He cut into the next lane, then the next. A horn blared—just missed him. Rhan swerved for the turn-off, spraying loose gravel on the shoulder of the road. But he'd made it. He pulled onto the first side street and stopped, the car idling. He turned the music off and the sudden silence was like a gaping hole. He was shaking.

He knew what he'd done was stupid, that it was dangerous, and not just for him.

But I'm not going to lose, he told the Universe. It's your game, but I'm playing to win. From now on, it's me first.

SIX

I N high school, Rhan had been anything from a fair to excellent student, depending on how interesting he found the class. But this was different, he told himself. Now it didn't matter how he felt. If it was learnable, he'd learn it.

It worked in the hard-wired classes: Television, Single Camera Production, Audio. This was equipment with buttons, and he'd always been good with controls. In Audio, he caught on fast. He loved the look of a step diagram, the complicated map of how power was channeled through the electronics board. It reminded him of a maze.

Audio trained them on all forms of recording equipment: CD, reel to reel and carts—the special cartridges that re-cued themselves automatically. When Rhan saw his first reel-to-reel machine, he almost laughed. Big, square, cumbersome, it had plastic take-up reels stuck on the front like eyes. It made him think of a robot from an old, bad movie.

And yet there was a sensitivity, he discovered, a hands-on closeness that the other machinery didn't have. To cue it, he had to manually turn both reels—the magnetic tape threaded through the playback head—and listen for the first sound. He liked to play with it. If he turned slowly, the sound stretched and distorted into a low rumble; if he ran it through fast, it chirped. It was like playing with time.

Bob Arnott was in the class with him, but they didn't pretend to be in the same group; that had ended in Studio A. Rhan discovered that Bob hadn't taken Audio in his pre-training at cable; they were both learning this from the ground up. It made every class an unspoken contest—which of them could learn faster, do the work better. They hardly talked and never worked as partners, but at the end of every assignment they had their most meaningful conversations, out in the hallway: How did you do?!

It was a challenge and a taunt, and it raised the stakes of every test.

Devon McGuinness was a Radio major, and being in second year, he was in the audio labs a lot. He did wicked impressions of their instructor, Bill Robertson, or at least he tried: he had to reach for notes so low they made him cough. Bill was silver-haired and straight-laced. Mr. Old-Time Radio, Devon called him, but his real nickname was Gold 'n' Gravel. He had a voice as deep as a chasm, with the trace of a raspy rumble. He makes the rest of us sound like chipmunks, Rhan thought.

Bill caught Devon once, entertaining four of them in one of the tiny audio labs. Rhan held his breath, but the instructor only dropped a hand on Devon's shoulder.

"Thirty-five years of cigarettes and whiskey," Gold 'n' Gravel intoned, "and you might be on your way."

As soon as Devon found out that Rhan was planning a TV Operations major, he began a mission to convert him.

"TV is yesterday's man, a flash in the pan, smoke and chroma-key," he'd say, his blue eyes twinkling. "Radio—now there's a bright future. Repent your sins and join us."

Rhan argued that he didn't have any sins worth repenting.

"See? Radio could change all that. You'd soon be guilty of plenty."

He made it sound almost tempting. Once, Rhan was dubbing a commercial in the lab, partnered with Amanda. Frizzy-haired and politically correct, she was a young woman who liked to argue. This time they couldn't agree on which speed to tape the copy at: 7 1/2 ips or 15 ips. The Irishman suddenly leaned in the open door.

"A gentleman gives a lady fifteen inches per second, or he's no gentleman at all," he cooed.

"Oh, grow up!" Amanda retorted, but Rhan was on the floor.

He wished all the classes were like that, but they weren't. Rhan discovered that when he moved away from hardware, he felt adrift. It was difficult to play to win in subjects that didn't always have right and wrong answers—Research Gathering, Interpersonal Skills, Advertising.

Research Gathering was like a current events course taken to the *nth* degree. Not only did they have to be aware of the news of the day, Tory Samuels tried to get them to anticipate it. Young, handsome and dark-skinned, he was the news director of a major radio station. At the beginning of every class, he'd shoot out a challenge at them: "What will be my three lead stories tonight?"

He wasn't looking for a psychic prediction. By following the news the night before and knowing which events were scheduled for the day—what was brewing, germinating—he felt they should get at least one or two right.

Rhan had a problem with the news. He didn't mind watching it on his tiny color portable. He was intrigued by the cuts and angles, and all the different ways there were to frame a face. But he watched it with the sound off. He found the voice-over distracting, and it was hard to believe that what happened in Somalia or Saskatchewan was going to make a difference to him. Even the local stories seemed far away. I know what my life is about, Rhan thought.

One morning Tory Samuels changed the question: "What will be my *top* story today?" The class threw back answer after answer—rumors of a provincial election, Canadian peacekeepers on trial, hundreds stranded by a freak storm in British Columbia—but Tory kept shaking his head.

"A man was beaten to death and thrown into the Bow River, half a block from a gay nightclub. That is my top story."

The classroom buzzed, confused. It was just another murder.

"Is it?" Tory said. He reminded them of news stories over the summer, of the growing and vocal commitment by the Aryan Alliance to unite the Christian Patriots, neo-Nazis and other racist groups into one tide of "leaderless resistance."

"By operating through 'phantom cells' without formal leaders, they're employing the protective technique that worked so well for the terrorists of the 1970s," Tory said. "No one person knows enough to endanger the whole group."

"What about the money?" Grant Nostecki said from the back of the room. Grant was always asking about money. He'd probably wind up with his own show, Rhan thought—Nostecki Knows Your Dough. "Nobody operates without money," Grant continued, "but cell groups aren't going to be good fundraisers. They're soldiers."

"Good question. I bet the RCMP ask themselves that every day," Tory said. "Money has to be channeled in and distributed out, but my hunch is that it's through a series of people. Again, very few individuals will be in the position to endanger the whole process."

"You're making a lot of assumptions," Amanda blurted out. "If no one is taking responsibility for the murder, you don't know that racists are behind it."

"The third W, Amanda. Where. The body was

65

found near a gay nightclub. Gays are the second favorite target, if not the first."

Rhan was checking his notes. "But it's still not going to affect a lot of people. So why…"

"Because it's horror," Tory Samuels said simply. "And it's in our back yard. That's always your lead."

Rhan felt a jab inside, anger and repulsion. But he kept his mouth shut and took the notes, like everybody else.

He didn't like Advertising, either. In eighteen years he hadn't given much thought to commercials. He had a mute button on his remote and a trigger finger when it came to the car radio. The bits that slid in past that seemed harmless enough.

But advertising, he discovered, was the science of need and desire. What images affected the central nervous system. What people wanted as groups or individuals. How quickly they became numb to an effect. He was astonished by how much was known about him—or anyone—and how much money was spent finding out. Market Research, they called it. It made Rhan feel as if he was being tracked.

"Listen, media *is* advertising," the instructor Meg Bovaine said cheerfully. She was sitting on top of her desk, feet swinging lightly underneath. "Regardless of what you produce—television, radio, news—it all comes down to the power of persuasion. You have to convince people to watch or listen to you, and you've got a bloody brief time to do it." Her feet stopped swinging and she leaned forward earnestly. "And in this industry, there's an eighty percent chance you'll work for advertising— or with it or around it. It pays to keep the station on air, it pays your salary."

Rhan didn't doubt that, but he couldn't make himself care, either. He struggled for an hour with the first radio commercial he had to write, and ended up with five words: *Please buy the damn car*. It made Meg laugh, even as she gave him an F.

"Resistance is futile," she said, still smiling. "You can hate it, pretend to ignore it, but advertising works. Even on you."

Jen was in the class, and somehow he always seemed to be sitting in the row next to hers. He was surprised that she hardly took any notes. Whenever he glanced at her she was sitting at the edge of her seat, leaning forward, rapt and still. As if, Rhan thought, she was absorbing the information into her skin.

He liked that skin, the color of it, the way it stretched over her wrists and ankles, her neck and face. If he didn't stop himself, he could imagine a whole lot more of it. No matter what she wore— jeans and sweatshirts, sweaters and leggings—there was something subtle and female that glimmered through, flashed at him like the slender gold chain around her neck.

Since that first day in the studio, they'd hardly spoken. She smiled politely in passing, but she never said it was time to buy her a shirt, or a drink. Rhan thought he knew why. He didn't know how much Jen had heard standing outside the studio, but a little would have been enough. Why spend time getting to know someone who'd be out by Christmas? Why bother with someone who didn't deserve to be there? Rhan had never seen determined effort like he saw around him at SAIT. There was a raw push forward and an unspoken current. This was about jobs, the future. He wasn't the only one racing with the Universe.

The day of the radio ad, he was surprised when she caught up with him in the hallway after class.

"How'd you do?" she asked.

Rhan straightened. With Bob Arnott that was a challenge. He didn't know what it meant now.

"Not bad." Then he grinned. "Actually—really bad."

"But it's so interesting," Jen said.

"For you, maybe."

"But it's just human nature," Jen said excitedly. "It's around you all the time. What do people want? Then, what do they *really* want? And how do you use that to get the response *you* want?"

"It's dishonest," Rhan blurted.

Jen laughed. "Then so are contact lenses and hair gel. That's not dishonesty, it's…seduction." She stepped in closer. He could almost sense the temperature rise in the air next to him. "And think about it. No one can sell you something you don't really want. Advertising doesn't work unless the basic desire is there in the first place, buried in the psyche."

"But that's just it," Rhan said. "All the basic desires *are* there, genetically programmed in. So it's not fair."

He was startled to feel her hand on his arm.

"We're in media," she whispered, teasing. "We're not supposed to use that word."

He watched her go, the elusive, swaying walk that only women had. But he couldn't go after her.

Once bitten, twice shy, Gran had always said. But he was a twice-bitten man and his heart was in exile, even though the rest of him kept going out.

J.R., his friend back in Thunder Bay, had a type: "Ass and long hair. I am a dead man for ass and hair." Rhan didn't think he had a type. He liked them all. There was hardly a look that didn't whisper to his body—bountiful women who filled out every seam, the lipstick and perfume girls, even the hard little chippies dressed in black, thin as pretty boys, gold rings through their ears and lips, every glance like a call, *Here and Now.*

Girls liked J.R. They wanted him, and sometimes that desire had spilled over and made opportunities for Rhan—few, brief and furtive. It made for one-night stands or left-over girls, the ones who'd come to the party hoping for J.R. but were a little drunk and pretty lonely by the end of the night. Sex had been like fast food, Rhan thought.

Something you really wanted, couldn't wait to have, but a half-hour later the experience was lead in your stomach. He wasn't aggressive, he wasn't unkind, but he hadn't been really noble, either. He gave nothing away—thoughts, even sounds locked up in his chest. It was a solitary experience, and not just for him.

The last time had been back in the spring. A black country road, the cramped back seat of the Mazda, windows blurred with steam. And finally, in the darkness that was supposed to be bliss, she said, "Are you still here? I can't tell."

And that was the end. Driving home alone, disgust carving out a canyon inside him, desperately wanting something else, something more. If that's all you're going to do, do it yourself. You know where it is. You won't hurt anybody then.

Love was a place where you could lay all your secrets down, Rhan thought, and he had never been there. But he wanted to. He wanted someone he could trust, who *liked* him, not just settled for him. He dreamed of love like a shelter; he would fight to protect the one who would protect him. But he wouldn't be the one who reached out first, not this time.

The first Sunday after he'd arrived in Calgary, Rhan did his laundry. He had a grasp of the concept. At the Trail's End, everyone pitched in to help with the constant stream of sheets and towels from the cabins. Rhan had always volunteered to fold because he could do it in front of the TV. If Gran insisted he wash his own clothes, he'd just wait in the laundry room for five minutes, then call, "What should I use to pack it down with? A hockey stick?" He'd be demoted back to folding.

Now, standing in the little laundry room that separated his suite from the upstairs of the house, Rhan realized he was not going to be rescued. Almost everything he owned was in piles at his feet, and he couldn't put this off any longer. But the machine gave him too many choices: three completely different cycles, eight temperature combinations. When he checked the tags inside the clothes, it only raised more questions. Was 40 degrees considered hot? What did that little hand in a bucket mean? And were the directions absolute, or just loose guidelines?

There was a faint clatter of pots above him. His landlords. He couldn't ask them because he hadn't introduced himself yet, hadn't even thanked them for making up the bed. He figured he'd do it when he gave back the sheets—clean—but that brought him back to laundry. It was a vicious cycle.

Just then the door at the top of the stairs opened. A pert woman grinned at him over the top of a heaped basket.

"Well, hi. I didn't hear the water running so I thought the washer was free."

Late forties, she looked like somebody's mom, not a witch. Her curly hair was cut short and she

71

had the husky healthiness of a farm wife. Still, she seemed to struggle with the basket as she brought it down the stairs, dropping it with relief on the concrete floor.

"Well, it almost is. I only have one load," Rhan said.

"Actually, that's three loads," she said, still smiling. "You know, this machine is old and a little tricky. Want me to run through the controls with you once?"

Her name was Charmaine and her laundry lesson was brief and kind: whites in hot, colors in cold, sheets and towels separate.

"And if you're ever unsure, just check the back of the box." She tapped the instruction guide. "Three temperatures, one detergent!" she added brightly, mimicking the commercial. They both grinned.

She wanted to help him with the first load and Rhan felt an uncomfortable clutch. His underwear was buried in this pile.

"No, really, it's okay."

Charmaine pushed in the dial to start the water. "Oh, let's just get the darks in." She grabbed a pair of his jeans, scattering several pairs of shorts. Rhan scrambled to scoop them up, then realized he'd made it worse—he'd be *holding* his underwear in front of a strange woman.

"You've got something in the pocket," Charmaine said. The pale blue paper caught and

72

unfolded as she pulled it out. It was the pamphlet the girl in army boots had given him outside the mall in Regina. He'd never even looked at it but now he read it over Charmaine's shoulder.

THE TRUE NORTH...
DO YOU LOVE YOUR COUNTRY BUT HATE WHAT YOU SEE HAPPENING TO IT?
DO YOU FEAR FOR YOUR FUTURE, YOUR LIVELIHOOD?
DOES INJUSTICE MAKE YOU ANGRY?
DO YOU WISH THERE WAS SOMETHING YOU COULD DO?
SO DO WE!
JOIN US AND MAKE A DIFFERENCE!

There were three addresses—Toronto, Regina and Calgary—but just then Charmaine folded the paper again and tossed it abruptly onto the dryer.

"Well, good luck," she said, but her smile was tight now. She turned for the stairs. Rhan felt a pang. He didn't know what had upset her but Charmaine was nice. He didn't want it to end like this.

"Uh...could you tell me one more thing?"

He pulled a shirt from the pile. The washer had begun its agitation with the lid up, and he had to raise his voice to be heard over the violent sloshing.

"What's this one mean?" he said, showing her the tag at the neck.

"Hand wash only," Charmaine said.

"Oh." Rhan hesitated, then glanced into the tub of churning water. "Don't they get sued for injury?"

Charmaine began to shriek. She clutched her side and stumbled to the stairs, leaning back against them. Rhan rushed over—but she was laughing!

"My stitches, my stitches!" she gasped, but she couldn't stop. And as he hovered over her, the door at the top of the stairs flew open.

"What's happened?! What's the matter?" She was tall and slender, with white skin and black hair pulled back into a tiny, taut bun. But the alarm in her face was clear.

"I'm all right, Claire-Marie. He just made me laugh," Charmaine panted. She struggled to get up and Rhan leaned in to help her.

"I had my gallbladder out, two weeks ago." She gripped his forearms to pull herself up. "Hurts like hell."

Starting up the stairs, she put her hand on his shoulder to steady herself, and gave it a little squeeze. Rhan felt the warmth inside.

When the door had closed, he stuffed the rest of the darks into the washer and picked up the blue pamphlet Charmaine had tossed aside. He wanted to read it again but he was swept up by brilliant images, more intense than any dream.

An ice palace, a fortress, sat on a night hill. Its opaque walls gleamed white in the moonlight but the balustrades were empty, unarmed. Not a soul walked to protect it. The Viking horde fell on it suddenly, savagely, rough men carried forward on a wave of hate and desire. They hacked at the walls with axes, laid blows with their blunt hammers, but they could not chip or dent the enchanted ice. And yet it was melting, from the inside. Without fire or sunlight the walls were growing thin, transparent, revealing to the wild men the prize inside—a treasure beyond price. The cry went up, lust and fury, as the Vikings threw themselves at the fortress, efforts redoubled.

On the horizon, there appeared a lone knight...

"No." Rhan said the word out loud. He was leaning against the dryer, shaken and dizzy. He'd forgotten what the visions were like, how he could feel them from the inside, too. Now he was fighting the rush of emotion—piercing sorrow and the need to protect a treasure that was not his own.

He didn't understand what he'd seen, but he didn't want to be that knight. He already had a cause.

"Me first," he told the Universe grimly, but he folded the pamphlet and put it in his pocket.

SEVEN

THERE were corners in your life, Rhan thought. There were long, slow paths that seemed to go on forever, and then there were abrupt turns that came out of nowhere, when a single step put you in another country. Rhan discovered his country was Single Camera Production.

Mark was the instructor for Single Camera as well as Studio, and Rhan had gone into the class taut with expectancy. He had to keep proving himself. But he was fascinated so quickly, so completely, that the worry fell away. Count Dracula could have been leading the group and it wouldn't have mattered.

The first few weeks they didn't touch a camera. The focus was on how to tell a visual story.

"The narration, the voice-over are important aspects of a production," Mark said, "but the pictures are the story. Sound, of any kind, is a special effect. That means the person with the camera is the storyteller, and that's a big responsibility."

He rested his foot on the desktop and leaned forward on his knee. "You put your perspective into the story, without a word, just by what you show and when. For example, do we see the kid grabbed by the cops and thrown to the ground...or do we see the first part, where he runs out of the convenience store, his arms full of stolen goods?"

The room was silent, taking it in. "Don't be mistaken. We're a suspicious, jaded culture. We know people lie. But we believe what the camera tells us, we believe what we *see*. That's a powerful thing to hold in your hands." Mark smiled faintly. "But ethics are in second year. Let's talk about storyboards."

Rhan was sitting still and quiet. He hadn't written down a single word. The information seemed to take hold at a subatomic level, a slow tingle rising up from the base of his spine. After all the classes in illusion—cardboard cityscapes, market manipulation—this man was telling them to be careful with the truth. That it was important, that it mattered.

One day Mark brought in video footage made by other First Years, simple stories in their roughest form: a guy asks a girl for a date, a cyclist challenges a car to a race. The tapes were silent chunks of footage, over-long and out of sequence. As a group, the class was to decide how the stories should be edited. Mark dimmed the lights and plunked the date story into the playback machine. Rhan began scribbling down the list of shots to work with later: *Guy sees girl, makes eye contact, walks over, girl turns away...*

"That's your first shot," Jen blurted.

The room burst into surprised laughter and Mark paused the tape. "Thank you, Madame Director," he said, grinning. "Why do you say that?"

"Because it starts the story," Jen said. She seemed embarrassed but determined. "The guy doesn't just walk over. Men are cowards. She sees him first, connects, then calls him over by turning away."

A young man named Jeff let out a moan. "Don't tell me I've been screwing up for twenty-four years."

"You've been screwing up for twenty-four years," Jen said cheerfully. The room laughed again.

"Give the lady a cigar," Mark called over the noise. "We must have re-cut this tape up a dozen times...and that's how we finally did it."

He pressed Play and the story continued. Rhan was facing the monitor but something made him glance over, to the right, just in time to see Jen look away.

In the middle of October, Rhan fell in love. She came dressed in black, with silver trim that was riveted at the corners. She weighed eighteen pounds and she glinted at him across the room. Larger and more complex than the camcorder he'd filmed his demo tape on, she was an elegant slip compared to the burly metal giants in the studio.

"Meet the JVC-KY27," Mark said, lifting the camera out of its large case. "Most of us just call it a BetaCam because that's the recording unit that fits into the back." A "dockable" camera, he explained, was a basic block of equipment that had its components attached or "docked" on, such as the lens, viewfinder and BetaCam. There was a deft sureness to the way Mark handled the camera, but also, Rhan thought, respect. He soon found out why.

"We only have two units for everyone in TV. If one of them is down with an injury, that's a real problem. Each of them is the price of a small car."

They spent a whole class taking turns docking the attachments and finally each had a chance to try it. Rhan waited impatiently, watching the awkward struggles as student after student shouldered the camera and strapped the weighty battery belt around his or her waist. Jen looked particularly unhappy.

"Wow," she said, as Mark helped her lift it off. "You feel kind of…trapped."

Rhan did not feel trapped. When the BetaCam was lifted onto his right shoulder, the weight was new, but not uncomfortable. He didn't even mind the belt studded with long, flat batteries, nick-named "chocolate bars." He wasn't running tape yet but as he positioned his eye to the viewfinder and the world came together in the magic frame, he felt a kick of excitement, even joy. This was right.

He began a slow turn, panning the room, and he heard Mark's voice, as if from another world.

"You have to get a feel for your dimensions," the instructor was saying. "It's like driving. You have to know where the edges of the vehicle are, and how fast you can move."

Rhan saw a blurred figure at the far edge of the room, and instinctively he reached to focus. They'd had no training on the controls but he guessed, and he guessed right. Jeff became clear, waving in the magic frame. "Hi, Mom."

Rhan had no idea how long his turn was. He kept moving, pulling image after image into view, a connection between his eye and hands that seemed to skip over conscious thought. Frame and focus, pan and zoom. At last he felt someone touch his left shoulder, gently, so he wouldn't be startled.

"Okay, Rhan," Mark said.

As he lifted the camera off and set it carefully onto a desk, he felt as if he was waking up. He noticed everyone was staring at him.

"First production, he is definitely my partner," Jeff said, and everyone laughed.

"No, mine!" someone else called.

"Great," Mark said, removing the lens. "A roomful of producers and one cameraman. You all have to learn this, people!"

A buzzer in the hallway sounded, ending the class. The room dissolved into noise as they began trooping out. Rhan was gathering up his module when Jen pulled in suddenly beside him.

"You made it look real," she whispered, sliding past and out the door. Behind him, Mark snapped the locks shut on the case.

"Good start," he said briskly, "but it's about more than metal."

From Mark Boutiniere that was dizzying praise, Rhan thought.

Calgary became a city on fire. The trees burst into yellow almost overnight and Rhan threw himself headlong into every golden day. He kept up his work in the other classes, but he knew it was bribery. When he loved, he loved completely. He lived for his three hours a week in Single Camera Production.

Meg Bovaine waggled her finger at him. "'Give everybody money' is not a sound basis for a campaign. What am I going to do with you?"

"Pass me on charm?" Rhan said hopefully. "On looks?"

Meg guffawed. "Nice try, but you're twenty years too late."

She let him rewrite anyway and he squeaked a pass.

In Audio, Bob Arnott managed a six out of seven on a manual editing task. "How'd you do?" he challenged in the hallway. Rhan began bowing as he backed away.

"You're the king," he said.

"What?" Bob said, confused and suspicious.

"All hail Lord Bob," Rhan said.

"What are you talking about?!" Bob called after him. But Rhan walked away, a free man.

The days sped on and he sped with them. Some mornings he even managed to beat the baby blue time bomb that ticked in his shower.

"I win," he'd say, slamming the button down with spiteful glee.

Mornings were getting chilly. He was always grateful to wrap his hands around the steaming cup as he walked out of the convenience store. Coffee worked for the body as well as the soul, Rhan thought. He tried not to glance at the store window around the corner, but some mornings he caught himself staring at the hammer. It made him think of Vikings, and ice melting without heat or light. It made him wonder what treasure was beyond price.

You know what treasure you're after, he told himself, shaking the vision off. You just have to dig it up.

Mark had been right, the class was about more than the equipment. There was a lot to learn: the pre-production work of storyboards, shot lists, narration. Afterwards there was sound work and editing. Like almost everyone else, Rhan let his shots go on too long; he didn't want to lose any of it. Mark finally sent Jen into the editing booth with him.

"Be brutal, Madame Director. Save him from himself," he said.

In the small room there was just space enough for two chairs, a table with a monitor, and two record and playback machines. Jen sat down beside Rhan, a stopwatch in her hand. He felt self-conscious. He was glad it was her but he didn't think he needed saving.

"You know, I can do this," he said, grinning.

Jen smiled back. "Sure. Run the tape."

It was a simple sequence. A cyclist puts on his equipment, mounts a bike and rides away. Everyone's tape was the same subject. The class had roped a second year Broadcast News student as their actor. Rhan let the silent tape run through and neither of them said a word. He was listening to her breathe, wondering if she liked it.

"That's great!" Jen said at the end.

"Yeah?"

"Yeah. Run it again."

He rewound proudly, eagerly. She watched for fifteen seconds, then said, "Okay, cut everything up to now."

"But that's my establishing shot!" Rhan sputtered.

"Okay, but establish the biker, not the trees. This isn't about trees," Jen said. Rhan grimly noted the tape time to edit later. The whole session was like that. Jen wasn't brutal but she was firm, and she had an instinct for what should happen and when. He argued some points—most of them—but in his guts Rhan had to admit she was usually right. As he worked he could feel the sequence becoming tighter, cleaner with every cut.

"Lose the leaf," Jen said at the end.

After his final long shot of the cyclist riding away, Rhan had focused on a leaf skittering across the pavement. It seemed to be a final statement. The more often he saw the tape, the more he liked it.

"No way," Rhan said. "It's great. I love the leaf."

They argued it out. Jen felt it wasn't important to the story; Rhan insisted that it was. And anyway, wasn't this his tape? The little room was heating up.

Suddenly Jen laughed. "Is this an artistic snit?"

Rhan felt the tension evaporate. "I'm holding out for creative control," he said, grinning.

"The leaf is *brilliant*," Jen said.

Out of the editing room, Rhan was sorry that it was over. It was his tape but it seemed that she cared. As if, Rhan thought, they'd been partners.

He got a 3.8 on the filming and a perfect 4 on the edit. He was jubilant as he thanked her.

"How'd you do on your tape?" he asked.

Jen shrugged and looked away. "I…Mark's going to let me re-shoot."

"Do you want some help?"

"No. I have to do this on my own. I have to learn this." She sounded determined, as if she was telling herself.

Their first major production assignment came at the end of October. The task was to create a visual map to SAIT, an introduction to the campus build-ings and areas.

"The purpose of this exercise is to bring the basic components together," Mark said. "You'll have the chance to write and film and edit the whole thing." He grinned. "It's sixty seconds that'll feel like a year."

As soon as he told them they'd be working in

teams, Jen leapt out of her desk and caught Rhan's arm. "I got him first!" she told the others triumphantly.

Rhan felt the wonder spread through his chest. Grabbing someone was like reaching out first, maybe?

He met her Thursday in the basement of H Building, at the equipment check-out, which was manned by a Second Year volunteer. Rhan and the checker went over the BetaCam point by point, confirming working order.

"If you're just on the campus, you don't need the case," the Second Year suggested. "It's really bulky to haul around. Just put the batteries and stuff in a camera bag."

Rhan felt a quiver of excitement as he loaded up the little bag, the size of a school backpack. It was thrilling to go out on their own, as if it was real, he thought.

"Okay," the Second Year said, thrusting the release form in front of him. "Sign your life away."

Rhan glanced at Jen. "Two hours?"

"Better make it an hour forty-five," the Second Year said. "I've got somebody booked in after you."

Outside on the campus, gold was gone, the trees stripped bare. The afternoon was crisp, bright but not glaring. Good light, Rhan thought.

He stopped abruptly. "Smoke," he said. The word seemed to come out on its own. He swung around, looking, and saw the black pillar rising and gathering in the sky. The SAIT administration building blocked his view but the fire had to be close, maybe just across the campus.

"It's the ACA," Jen said. She looked at him, brown eyes into his blue, a question they both knew the answer to.

They leapt off the mark in the same instant. Rhan jogged carefully with the camera, eighteen pounds of pure gold, but an electric current was running through him: Play to win.

The parking lot of the Alberta College of Art was a swirling sea of people, huddled in groups or walking around, looking at the others who continued to pour out of the building. An alarm clanged dully in the background.

"Okay." Jen was twisting in a circle, trying to see everything at once. "Okay. Let's get some shots, crowd shots..."

"The fire trucks, when they get here," Rhan said.

"Yeah, the trucks." There was a tremor in her voice. She was as excited as he was. "I can't remember. Do we have sound?"

"Not a separate feed. But I can get it on the tape," Rhan said.

"Okay. I'm going to find somebody who knows something." Jen squeezed his arm suddenly. "Don't go anywhere, unless you have to," she said, then darted into the crowd.

For a moment Rhan felt caught in a windstorm,

buffeted by sounds and images. This wasn't the studio or even class. What was he supposed to do first?

Get the tape into the camera, stupid. He dropped to one knee and opened his camera bag, rummaging for tape and batteries. His hands were shaking. This was real. What if he did it wrong, missed something? He strapped on the belt and hoisted the BetaCam onto his shoulder but hesitated, wondering how to frame his first shot. The distant cry of sirens seemed to shoot straight up through his ribs.

Don't get fancy, Van. Just get it.

He got it—the flashing trucks as they pulled up, the firefighters and their deft, drilled position, big boots pounding on the pavement. There was a young woman in a sweater standing alone, hugging herself in the chilly air, and he got that, too.

The confusing windstorm was gone. Looking through the lens, concentrating on one thing at a time, he moved from shot to shot in a fluid dream. And there was something else—not vision, not sound, but a sense of space, Rhan thought. What Mark had said about knowing his dimensions—only a step farther. He could back up and turn without bumping into anyone. He just knew where people were.

He was lowering the camera when Jen came running up.

"All right," she said breathlessly, "I've got the director of Fine Arts. He'll give us a quote."

They set up with a fire truck as a backdrop. Around them, the emergency seemed to be winding down. Smoke was still gathering in the sky but it was more gray than black. Before he began to shoot, Rhan caught a glimpse of the firefighters trailing out of the building.

Jen was good. She insisted Rhan go for a head-and-shoulders shot of the director, cropping her out of the frame, but her questions led the story out of the man easily: the fire had started in A-Wing and although no one knew the cause yet, evacuation had been quick and easy; the new sprinkler system had probably diverted most of the damage.

It wasn't a big deal, as fires went. But it's ours, Rhan thought stubbornly. A red light began to flash in the corner of his viewfinder—only a few minutes of tape left.

And then he began to feel it, a buzzing behind him and to the right. It wasn't a sound but a sensation, and it was getting stronger. He swung around, tape rolling.

Through the lens he saw a small annex next to A-Wing, a single-story addition that reminded him of the portable units at his old high school. There was no one nearby. It was quiet, white and square.

"Rhan?!" Jen said. "We're not fin…"

A low sonic rumble cut her off and the annex windows blew out, gushing orange and black.

EIGHT

"OH, my God!" Jen blurted. She was hanging onto the shoulder strap of her seatbelt as the Mazda hurtled through rush-hour traffic. Rhan saw an opening in the next lane—there wasn't time to signal.

"My God!" Jen said again.

"What time is it?" Rhan asked. He had a watch but he wanted to take her mind off the traffic, and the way he was driving through it.

"Almost ten to six."

"The office will probably be closed but the news director will stay until after the six o'clock cast," Rhan said. "We'll just bang on the door until somebody lets us in." He changed lanes again. "If I really got it, it's a great piece of tape."

"No, it's an *incredible* piece of tape," Jen said. "How much did you get after the explosion?"

"Maybe a minute." A minute of pandemonium, the time it took flames to engulf the annex. No one had been hurt but it was the shock, Rhan thought. Even to him. He had run out of tape but he would have stood there, staring with everyone else, if the Channel 9 news cruiser hadn't pulled up. That had given him an idea.

"Dear Jesus!" Jen whispered, as the Mazda careened around a corner. She glanced into the back seat where the BetaCam was strapped in with a seatbelt.

They pulled into the Channel 2 parking lot on the stroke of six. When they burst into the front office, the receptionist already had her coat on. She called the news director, Willie Shine, and then left them standing there as she went out. There was a television monitor positioned in a high corner, just below the ceiling. Silent and brilliant in the dim room, the six o'clock newscast had just started. Rhan paced restlessly; Jen stood with her arms crossed tightly over her chest. At last Willie Shine shambled into the reception area.

He would have been tall but his broad-shoul-dered frame was stooped, weary. A cigarette dan-gled from his fingers, the smoke trailing up tanta-lizingly in the polished glass room.

"We don't buy much freelance," the news direc-tor said, after Rhan briefly explained who they were and what they had. "And I heard about it on the police band anyway—not much of a fire."

"Until the explosion," Rhan said.

Willie Shine perked up. "Explosion? You got it?"

"We sure did," Jen cut in, "and Channel 9 didn't."

The director took the tape to preview—he was almost hurrying. He didn't bring it back.

"We'll use it on the eleven o'clock cast," he said, and named a sum worth two days' pay at the mill. Rhan hung onto the edge of the reception desk, try-ing to keep his feet on the floor.

Jen insisted the check go out to Rhan, and Willie

Shine recorded his address in a battered log book. Finishing, he looked up.

"That's a phenomenal shot. How'd you know it was going to blow?"

Jen turned to look at Rhan, curious, as if she'd just thought of that, too.

"I…heard something," Rhan shrugged. There was a second's silence, then the news director laughed, a nervous snort.

"Well, it didn't pick up on tape."

At the door, letting them out, he held out two business cards, one for each of them.

"If you get something, call me any time," Willie Shine told Rhan.

As soon as he was gone, Rhan leapt down the eight stairs onto the pavement.

"YESSS!"

Jen came down after him slowly. Her smile looked tight.

"I'm glad for you," she said. "This is…thrilling."

"For you, too," Rhan said. He was perplexed. She didn't sound thrilled. "Half the money's yours. I'll give it to you as soon as I…"

Jen shook her head. "I didn't *do* anything."

"That was a great interview…"

"They're not going to use it," Jen argued. "Weren't you listening? Your shot was what he wanted. That's what he paid for."

"No, we're partners." Rhan held up the business card. "Hey, I'll phone him, tell him he's got to…"

"Don't you dare!" Jen sputtered, angry now. "Don't you dare humiliate me."

"I'm not. But we're partners," Rhan insisted. "This...belongs to both of us."

"No, it doesn't. It's yours. Will you just enjoy it!" She wiped at her face suddenly. "And will you please open this car?"

Rhan stared, dumbfounded. She was crying?

"Now?!"

Rhan unlocked the Mazda. They both got in but he didn't start it. His mind was racing. What had he done? What had he said? And what was he going to do now?

She wasn't crying loudly. She was staring straight out through the windshield.

"This is so embarrassing," Jen said fiercely, wiping at her face with a tissue. "Really, it's not like me."

"Okay," Rhan said.

"I mean, it's stupid." Her voice quavered. "I get the best cameraman in first year, we get this incredible tape, but...it's not *me*. So I sit in his car and bawl?! Jenny, you're stupid!"

"No, you're not," Rhan said.

"Anything mechanical, I'm failing it," she said grimly. "I can't film a thirty-second bike ride, I can't remember how to set tone and bars in the studio from one day to the next. Talk about not deserving to be here."

That hurt. It brought his first day in the studio rushing back in his face.

"So you heard," Rhan said.

"Heard what?" She looked at him, her tear-streaked face suddenly fearful. "What are they saying about me?"

For an instant he was silent, astonished. She *didn't* know, but how was he going to get out of this? He grappled for a lie but she was watching him intently. This mattered.

"Mark said I didn't deserve to be here," Rhan said finally. "That he'd burn me out by Christmas."

"You?! I don't believe it. You're the Boy Wonder. You can do anything."

Rhan felt a flutter at the compliment. "It's true. He told me the first class in Studio. Now, *that* was a great day," he said, grinning.

Jen let out a breath that was almost a laugh. "And I thought it was just me."

"Why? What did he say?"

"Nothing. But I'm sure he thinks the same thing, that I'll be out by Christmas. I'm sure they all think it."

"Why?"

She glanced at him hesitantly, deciding.

"I'm here on this sort of…grant," Jen started. The Alberta Metis Foundation was paying her way through the program.

"But that's great," Rhan said. "That's like a scholarship."

"Oh, yeah, a scholarship. As long as your family has been on welfare for three generations," she said bitterly.

"So who cares where the money comes from," Rhan said. "You made it, like everybody else."

"No, I didn't," Jen said. She was looking at her hands in her lap. "I got the Sorry-try-again-next-year letter. I was upset, yeah, but my…grant consultant was really mad. Two weeks later I get another letter that says I'm on the waiting list. Then after that, I get accepted."

The air in the car seemed very close. He knew this was a secret.

"You won't fail," Rhan said. "You're too good."

She looked at him, cautiously hopeful. Rhan rushed on, reminding her how well she did in Advertising, Presentation, Research and Information Gathering. Some things he only guessed at, but she didn't argue.

"And," Rhan steeled himself, "you were right about the leaf. I should have cut it."

Jen laughed. "Now that takes guts. You deserve a prize or something."

Rhan's heart quickened. "Okay. You want to do dinner?"

She did. They went to a drive-through and parked, the smell of onion rings stamping itself on the car's interior forever. Jen was worried that they hadn't done the filming they were supposed to, for the assignment. Rhan argued that what they had done was more important, and that they'd get another chance.

"It's what they're training us for, right? To go

94

out in the world. We just went early."

Jen took a bite of her burger, chewing thoughtfully. "You really think my interview was good?"

"It was great," Rhan said.

"Do you think they'll use...even maybe a bit of it?"

"Yes," he said. *Please*, he begged silently—him, who was at war with the Universe. But this wasn't for him.

It was nine o'clock by the time they were finished. They decided to watch the eleven o'clock news together, to see their clip.

"At your place?" Rhan asked.

"Oh, no," Jen said quickly, then shrugged a little nervously. "It's just so full there. My sisters, their kids. Babies everywhere. The news isn't a big deal," she finished, an edge to her voice.

"Well," Rhan took a breath, "there's my place."

Jen looked at him, grinning but cautious. "Let's go shopping."

"What?"

"You owe me a shirt, and we've got two hours," she said cheerfully.

Rhan groaned as he fired up the engine. All the stores were closed, but Jen hadn't planned on getting out of the car anyway. They drove around under the bright lights, past the shiny glass-and-marble stores, Jen playfully trying to steer him past the most expensive shops, him trying to avoid them.

"Hmm. Turn right. Aylene's House of

Outrageous Couture is around the corner."

"Dive! Dive!" Rhan cried, swerving left.

It was fun. He'd driven around these streets so many times, but it was different with someone else. Especially this someone. The sadness and anxiety had passed; her voice lit up the car. But he thought about the other moment, too, what it had been like to hear a secret, and tell one. It changed the air, Rhan thought.

They went to his place before eleven. Fumbling with his keys in the dark outside his suite, Rhan wondered if he was allowed to have people in. Better keep the noise down, just in case.

Inside, he snapped on the lights and the carnage hit him full in the face: a jacket on the kitchen table, pizza boxes on the floor, pop bottles jostling for space with the dirty dishes on the counter. Imagining it through Jen's eyes made it even worse.

He turned. "Oh, my God, I've been robbed! Look—they trashed the place."

"Then they were here for at least five meals," Jen said wryly, glancing around.

Rhan grinned and kicked off his runners. "You wait here. I'll look around, make sure it's safe."

In the living room he grabbed armfuls of dirty laundry off the couch, thankful that he didn't have it pulled out as a bed. But even that brief thought brought a flush of heat to his face. He tried to organize the other debris and noticed the red message light blinking on his answering machine. Zoe, he thought, switching it off. He'd listen later. He had a girl he liked in his apartment. He couldn't think of anything more important than that.

He headed back to the entrance. "They put up a fight but it's…"

Jen started. She dropped his runner and stood up guiltily from where she'd been crouched on the floor.

Rhan was surprised. "What? What's with my shoes?"

Jen laughed, girlish and embarrassed.

"They're not cross-trainers or anything," Rhan shrugged.

"I…like them," Jen said softly.

He stepped closer, intrigued. "Why?"

She hesitated, still smiling shyly, then dropped to one knee. "Men's shoes are so different." She picked up the runner again. "They're so…blunt. Forceful. Look at the toe, it's wider than my fist. And the treads, they're huge."

Rhan crouched beside her. He thought about shoes for about thirty seconds twice a year, when he bought them. But he was caught up in the hushed, intimate sound of her voice. She was telling him another secret.

"And they're heavy," Jen said. "Look." She squirmed to take off one of her own shoes and held it in her other hand, comparing them. Flat-heeled brown suede, it had three gold squares across the top. It was so small and sleek next to his.

She looked at him, a sideways glance. "You think I'm nuts."

"No." He took the brown shoe from her. Still warm from her foot, it was so narrow he could have closed his hand around it. He ran his thumb across the suede, entranced by the sensation.

"I have a friend," Jen said dreamily, still studying his runner. "She likes guys in cowboy boots. But to me, this is just so…male. You don't even untie the laces."

He wanted to kiss her, a lot. He wanted to kiss her lips and the bare neck he'd stared at so many times. He wanted to put his cheek against her hair, to hold her and be held. He wanted…

"It's all women in my house," Jen said. She put down his runner and stood up. "Smart women making stupid choices."

…to be faster, Rhan thought in dismay. He got up carefully.

They sat on the couch in front of Rhan's small TV. Jen was on the edge of the seat, leaning forward, her hands clasped together nervously. News of the world seemed really unimportant right now.

"The Alberta College of Art was rocked by an explosive fire today…"

Jen seized his hand and hung on. Brief two-second cuts of the building, the smoke, the trucks—his shots. Rhan couldn't stop the rush of excited pride.

"The fire seemed well under control…" the newscaster said.

"…I believe most of the damage has been diverted," the director of Fine Arts was saying. There was the sudden, dizzying slide of images that settled on the annex. For a long single second the image held, then came apart. Even though he'd known it was coming, Rhan seemed to feel the explosion in his chest. He understood the look on Willie Shine's face. The delay was…eerie.

Jen jumped up with an excited shriek. "We did it—I did it! They used it!"

Rhan got up and was nearly knocked off balance as she threw her arms around him.

"One whole sentence, but they used it." She kissed him. "Thank you! I wasn't even going to watch. But you made me believe…" She didn't finish but kissed him again and he met her, ready this time. The heat that had barely died down rose up in a flare.

"You deserved it," Rhan panted, when they pulled apart for air. "It was a great interview…"

And then they stopped talking. His glasses were in the way; he took them off. He was touching and holding and inhaling her, his face in her fragrant hair, her breath in his ear. Her hands slipped up under his shirt, hot and human against his back, pulling him in tightly. His heart was pounding. This wasn't fast food. He liked Jen, he really liked her. She was smart and fun and exciting to work with, and they had each given up a secret. It seemed welded together: the rush of this incredible day and his future soaring out in front of him; the heat of her body against him now.

The pendant on her chain was a cross. The clasp on her bra was in the front. He unhooked it with a fumbling twist, and heard his own breath surge out in an urgent voice. He was hurting to have her, and his clothes were painfully in the way. He groped for the edge of his T-shirt, wondering if there was a way to pull it over his head without taking his mouth from her skin.

Jen pulled back. "I…I think we should stop."

"What?" Rhan gasped. "Why?"

"It was a great day. Exciting. *You're* exciting…" she hesitated. "But I only love people I love."

He was grappling with desperate hope. "I'm really lovable," he said.

She stepped back now, buttoning up her clothes.

"So prove it," Jen said. "Let's date or something. Okay?"

Her hair was tousled, bewitching. He wanted to touch it, brush it away from her face, but he didn't.

"Okay," Rhan said.

She wouldn't let him drive her home; the C-Train was half a block from his suite. He would have taken her there but she shook her head.

"No, I think I just want to…walk. Cool down."

He didn't know what expression was on his face, but at the door she kissed him suddenly. "Don't worry. You're the best fire of the day." She grinned. "I'll see you tomorrow. Wear your runners."

When she was gone he leaned against the wall, still shaken by the desire and disappointment. But underneath that he was amazed. It had been a long time since he'd been glad to be in his life. It was humbling.

Thanks, he told the Universe.

Now he only had technical difficulties. "Cool down," he whispered out loud. He wandered into the living room, turned off the TV and remembered the phone message. That would do it. Zoe was like a cold shower, he thought, hitting the Playback button.

"Yeah, Rhan, this is Mark. It's eight o'clock and I don't know where the hell my camera is." Pause. "Your ass is grass."

NINE

MARK'S office was small. There was barely space for a desk and the filing cabinet piled with video tapes. The walls were papered with notices and schedules, and a single quote in computer print-out: *A professional is someone who does his job well, even when he doesn't feel like it.*

No one was sitting. Jen stood with her arms crossed over her chest. Rhan was across from Mark, the desk between them.

"You're lucky I didn't call the cops. What have we been pounding into you guys from the first day? Take care of the equipment!"

"The camera was fine. I strapped it in with a seatbelt," Rhan said.

"So what if someone had sideswiped you on the road? Out of its case, it would have been destroyed. We're not insured for that. Or what if it had been stolen?"

"It was locked in my trunk overnight," Rhan cut in.

"So how was I supposed to know that? As far as I knew, twenty thousand bucks went out the door and you went with it. You signed your name, but it's my ass on the line for the equipment."

"Look, I'm sorry. But we were responding to the moment. Isn't that what this is all about?" Rhan gestured to include the school. "You see something and you react. We got the story and we got it on air…"

"I'm thrilled for you," Mark snapped. "But what about the people who had that camera booked after you? What did they get?"

Rhan felt a pang. He'd forgotten all about that.

"We should have run it back to the check-in," Jen said.

"Yeah, you should have," Mark said. "If you had, I would have let you re-book then, re-shoot the assignment."

"You have to let us re-shoot," Rhan cut in. Beside him he heard Jen inhale a sharp breath.

"No, I don't. What you did was stupid and thoughtless—grade school. That's an F."

"Please!" Jen blurted. "The camera's safe and we'll find the people we messed up…we'll apologize…"

Her tone bothered Rhan. With any other instructor in any other class he would agree with her. But Mark had been out to get him. He'd never had a chance. "Don't grovel to this guy, Jen. He likes to play it but he's not God."

"And you have an attitude problem."

"Rhan, we screwed up. Why are you fighting this?"

"Because I hate a bully."

"Do you want an F for the term, too?" Mark said evenly. "Is that what you're shooting for?"

Rhan looked at Jen.

"We'll take this up with somebody—Head of Communications. He can't do this!"

"Jen," Mark said, "I can get you in with another group. Ian and Jeff need the help."

Her face was taut. It was hard to imagine he had touched that face, kissed it. She glanced from Mark to Rhan to Mark again, and then the cluttered bulletin-board of a wall.

"Okay."

A single word. Like a gunshot. Rhan fumbled with the doorknob behind him. Mark stepped from behind the desk, his face softening for the first time.

"It's not about skills, Rhan. It's not about tape. You've got an attitude and you know what? It doesn't work."

Rhan was in the hall. He was walking.

"I've seen it before—and it doesn't work!" Mark's voice rang down after him in the empty corridor.

◆

The stairwell was narrow and dim; it smelled of decaying wood. He had driven past the old building twice before finding it. It looked as if it had once been a warehouse or showroom, with offices up top. It was a rarity in Calgary—something old that hadn't been torn down yet. On the fringes of downtown, it seemed far away from civilization. Rhan was glad.

He felt so betrayed. All he wanted was to find his place, something he could succeed at. He'd put his heart into Single Camera Production and he'd been getting ready to do the same with Jen, and they'd both abandoned him, turned on him. So here he was on unfamiliar streets at night, in a rickety old building, looking for the only other treasure he knew about.

He didn't know what he expected to find but the vision had made him feel there was something waiting for him at the True North. Maybe they were his group, his kind.

Just go and see, he'd told himself. You can always leave.

At the top there was a hallway of doors, and not all had numbers on them. But one did. Rhan took a breath and knocked.

The young man who opened it had a hard face and hair like a dark fuzz over his head. He was wearing a white T-shirt and khaki pants, the military look Rhan remembered from Regina.

"Yeah?"

"Is this the True North?" Rhan said.

The young man looked him up and down.

"I got a pamphlet," Rhan said, "with this address. A hand-out."

"Not lately you didn't," the man said. He was closing the door.

"Let him in, Conlan," a voice rang out behind, deeper in the room. Conlan glanced irritably over his shoulder, but the door swung open anyway.

The other man was sandy-haired and taller, with the kind of shoulders fashion magazines liked to hang expensive suits on. He was wearing a sports-coat without a tie, and sun-lines creased his face. Rhan guessed he was about the same age as Mark Boutiniere, nudging forty, but time had been kinder to him. Time and money.

They were in another short hallway, with just enough room for a table. On it was a clipboard and a jar marked "Donations." It was stuffed full of money, none of it coins. Farther down, Rhan could see another open door, crowded with people and folding metal chairs.

"Forgive the security," the man said. "Our meetings have been closed to the general public for a couple of months. But if you sign in," he gestured at the clipboard, "you're welcome to stay." His hand came out to Rhan. "I'm Jim Rusk."

He said it as though it should mean something. Rhan shook his hand but he didn't offer his own name. Caution was quavering in him like a bare wire. He'd thought this would be a sort of political group, or action committee. Why would the meetings be closed?

Jim Rusk strode off down the hall, toward the crowded room. Rhan bent over the clipboard, thinking fast. *Moe Gervais*, he wrote, and gave the street address of SAIT. It was a big campus.

Conlan had been watching him, reading over his shoulder, but now he shifted slightly, so that he was in Rhan's way. Defiantly, Rhan stuffed five dollars into the donations jar and shouldered past him.

The walls of the second room seemed strangely bare and discolored in places, as if pictures had been taken down. Rhan soon saw that a move was imminent; boxes set along the wall were filled but open.

There was a lectern at the front of the room and folding metal chairs facing it. Some people were sitting but most of the twenty-five or thirty were clustered in groups. There were a few suits and occasional leather but the vast majority wore the white and khaki like a uniform. Not military, Rhan thought, trying to place where he had seen that look. Survivalists? He'd read about those people who liked to rough it in the wilderness as they prepared for the end of the world. It was then that he realized there were only two women in the group, but with their shaved heads and hobnail boots it was an honest mistake.

Everyone was noticing him. Rhan felt the suspicious glance at least twenty-five times. From the right, the tail-end of a conversation floated over.

"…and the judge says, What do you have to say? And I said that it was fucking worth it!" Laughter.

That's when he saw the swastika. It was pinned to a suit lapel. Rhan felt the punch of heat and sudden alarm. He looked around the room intently and counted eight more—on shoulders and shirt fronts; one dangled from an ear. These weren't survivalists and it wasn't his group. Really not his group.

He turned out through the door, his stomach

churning, his mouth full of bitter spit. He felt tricked. He'd had hope in this.

Conlan grabbed his shoulder.

"Lose your balls, little man?" he said.

Rhan's arm flew up, breaking the hold. "Screw you," he said. It was the wrong thing. Conlan caught him before the end of the hallway, a hard shove from behind that sent him through the door and into a terrifying stumble down the stairs. He slipped and rolled, blow after blow against his back and shoulders, a whirl that ended in a solid slam into the wall at the bottom.

Rhan's head was spinning, but he grabbed the door handle to pull himself up. Get out, stupid! Too late—they were thundering down the stairs. Conlan was not alone now. Rhan swung out wildly, hoping to shove them away and get out the door. Someone caught his arm expertly and kicked his feet out from under him. In a half second he was on the floor again, arms wrenched behind him, a knee in his back.

Someone grabbed his ponytail, yanking back his head.

"Give me a knife," Conlan said.

Oh, God. His hair, or worse.

"Let him go!"

The cry shot through Rhan; it seemed to come from the top of the stairs. He was still held tight, but he tried to twist his head to listen.

"I said, let him go!" There was the solid tromping of boots down the wooden stairs and a sudden shuffle. Release. Rhan flipped over and scrambled to his feet.

Sweating, heart pounding, he looked into the surprised face of Lee Dahl.

Three years had not dimmed the Iceman. If anything, time had strengthened his face, squared his features into bolder lines. The once-bleached hair had grown out into its natural color, a dark blond too short to need a comb. He was still lean but broader across the shoulders, wiry force that showed clearly through the white T-shirt. In his khaki pants and hobnail boots, he looked like the others, or they looked like him.

"The faggot should die," Conlan said.

"Shut up." Lee didn't even turn his head. "He walks." He said it like an order, as if he was used to giving them. He pushed open the door and no one stopped him. Rhan walked.

He gulped the night air as if he'd been drowning. As soon as the door clanked shut behind him he was running. He sprinted to his car parked alone at the end of the street, made his trembling hand shove the key in the door lock. He swung in behind the wheel and started the engine.

A sudden flash of white thumping on the driver's window made him jump.

"Open up! I need to talk to you!" Lee's voice was muffled through the glass. Rhan kicked the gas. The Mazda surged forward; he swerved into the street. Thank God there was no one in front of him. He didn't look in the rearview mirror.

It took four blocks before he realized he couldn't see, that the street signs and stoplights were dangerously blurred. He reached for his glasses—still there. By a miracle they had survived, intact and in place. But he stared in disbelief at the wet side of his palm that had brushed against his face.

TEN

HE didn't cry at the hospital, he didn't cry at the funeral. He felt as if everyone was watching him, a man on his own, and that thought kept him moving, walking and breathing. It kept him upright.

"How're you doing?" Zoe asked him, all the time.

"I'm okay," Rhan said. He had lived in this woman's house for almost three years and they'd had some pretty good fights. Suddenly he felt absolutely driven to be polite.

"If you ever want to talk—" Zoe started.

"No, I'm okay," Rhan said.

"You're grinding your teeth at night," she said once, gently.

He felt himself straighten. "I'll...try to stop."

He went to work. With a little help from his friend J.R., he got on at Dominion Paper. J.R. hadn't worked there for a year, but he still knew people. And he knew the ropes.

"Don't take shit, but don't ask for it, either," J.R. said. "The guys on the loading dock are the worst. They're pretty bored."

"Okay," Rhan said. He was in this to make money. He figured he could keep his mouth shut and stay out of trouble for a few months.

"And watch where you sit in the lunchroom,"

J.R. said. "It's all kinda figured out. Everybody's got their own section."

"Okay," Rhan said.

"Fridays after work, everybody goes to the Crosstown." J.R. hesitated. "Don't go, bud."

Rhan had seen that bar, a long, low, flat building that looked like a plant itself. Even with the neon it was spartan, industrial.

"Why not?"

"The CP guys go there, too."

Rhan understood. J.R.'s cousin, Reine Dahl, was Lee Dahl's older brother and he worked for CP mills. J.R. hadn't spoken to Reine in over two years, ever since Rhan had shot the videotape of Reine beating Lee at a party. A lot of people in the family didn't talk to Reine anymore, J.R. said.

"Okay," Rhan said.

To the union at Dominion Paper, Rhan was considered general labor. The nice ladies in the front office called him a sweeper. To everyone else he was a Grunt. A Grunt did the jobs that no one else had designation for, or simply didn't want to do. If a single item weighed over seventy-two pounds, it legally didn't have to be carried by human hands. But there were a lot of things in the world under seventy-two pounds, Rhan discovered, and they all had to be moved somewhere. And he learned fast that they laughed if you got a dolly for anything under sixty pounds.

"Jesus, kid. Grow some balls and just carry it."

So he carried it—tools, boxes, supplies—swearing under his breath, sweat streaming under his navy coveralls. Rhan wasn't the only sweeper but he was the newest, and that made him the Grunt of Choice. The first two months at Dominion he barely swept at all. He went home hurting, muscles like burning welts along his back and arms and legs. When he woke up the pain was dimmer, but still there.

You're getting out, he told himself. Of the mill, of this city. You can do it because you don't have to do it forever.

He wasn't the only one who knew that. The skilled trades, the line workers, the heavy-equipment operators all knew he was just summer help, and it made a difference. In the lunchroom, sweepers always sat with the warehouse guys. Rhan sat alone at the far end of the table and ate his brownbag lunch, listening to the easy talk and sudden laughter far down to his right. If there hadn't been a name tag on his uniform, no one would have known what to call him.

One time the conversation turned to university. Bill Grant was talking about how many well-educated people had returned to the mill. "Stupid buggers came out with a Ph.D. and no J.O.B.," he said. "We've got the smartest damn warehouse in the province." Bill Grant was a square-shouldered forklift operator. At thirty he'd already been with Dominion ten years.

"Hey, you're going to some kind of college this fall, aren't you?"

Bill Grant was leaning forward, looking down the table at him. Rhan was surprised that the others were looking, too.

"Yeah," he said, and he couldn't help the little burst of pride. "I'm taking TV—"

"Well, shit," Grant cut him off. "I've been taking that for years. Three, four hours a night."

The table erupted into laughter and Rhan grinned along with them, but inside he was thinking, That was your moment in the sun, Grunt. Hope you enjoyed it.

It was a summer of long days and longer nights. It seemed to Rhan that after graduation, everyone he knew got jobs or got out of Thunder Bay. It was a city of strangers.

Then on a payday Friday at the end of August, Bill Grant asked him to a party. "No big deal, kid. Just a bunch of us. Somebody's birthday."

They were at the lockers; Rhan had changed back into his real clothes, his pay check folded up in his back pocket.

"The Crosstown?" he asked, trying not to let the caution surface in his voice.

"No, my house," Bill said, and he grinned. "Come on. We worked you harder than any other three guys. You deserve to cut loose."

Rhan suddenly wanted to go. He was eighteen

and it was Friday night and there was nothing waiting for him at the Trail's End.

"Yeah, sure," he said.

He took his own car. After a stop at the bank and
the liquor store he was on his way, steering the
Mazda into the lines of traffic that looked suddenly
bright against the darkening night. He couldn't
help running the words through his head, how he'd
worked harder than any three other guys.

Maybe this was how it always happened, Rhan
thought. Maybe they dumped on everybody new
and you just had to tough it out—"Grow some balls
and carry it." As he pulled up to Bill Grant's
rugged bungalow, grabbed his half-case off the seat
and started for the house, he thought that maybe
before the summer was out he'd even make it to the
Crosstown.

The blast caught him as he turned the dark corner into the back yard, sent him staggering on a
wave of shock and pain. He seemed to land against
something soft that shoved him forward again, into
the second slam, an explosion of jagged light. And
when the big man reached down and yanked him to
his feet and Rhan saw who it was, the fear and fury
seemed to burst in his veins. He began swinging like
a madman and he connected—once, twice—the
months of lifting at the mill caught his opponent by
surprise. He surprised himself.

But it was not magic. It wasn't the rush of blue
lightning the Universe gave him when somebody

else needed saving. Rhan was outweighed and out-numbered. Dimly he realized he was surrounded and he knew most of the faces. And they weren't going to help him.

A huge knee slammed his stomach and brought him to his knees, almost retching in pain. He felt the blast of a cowboy boot against his back, his ribs, his shoulder, and inside he was screaming, *Make it stop, please, make it stop!* When it was over, when he was just lying there, gasping and shaking, he heard Bill Grant's voice from the back of the little crowd.

"Happy birthday, Reine."

ELEVEN

WHEN Rhan woke up, the sky he could see through the narrow basement window was flat and gray. Winter was coming. He hadn't set the alarms because his first class wasn't until eleven A.M. But he'd had a restless sleep, waking up half a dozen times, the moments of real night and the dark of his dreams sliding into one another.

This isn't your fault, he told himself. You don't have to carry this.

But it was hard not to feel the weight of it. Three years ago, he had been the one who'd kept Lee Dahl from shooting his brother with a hunting arrow. He'd taken the arrow himself, in his own wrist. He'd kept Reine alive and Lee out of jail.

But who did you save? he asked himself. You saved a violent man so he could live to punish you. You saved his brother so he could run with dangerous people, become a big shot and maybe do more damage than you'll ever know.

The Universe was laughing in his face again. Proof, if he needed it, that there was no Magic Nation, no place where heroes lived. And at the center of the swirl of horror and sadness and guilt was a cold kernel: until last night he would have called Lee Dahl his friend. But he wasn't friends with racists, even with one who'd saved him from the others.

He sat up and headed for the shower, wincing as all his bruises made themselves known. There was only one place to go, and that was back into his life, in a hurry. He knew what he had to do today and it wasn't going to be fun.

He was locking his door when he noticed Charmaine in the laundry room, loading wet towels into the dryer. In a pink velour sweatsuit, she reminded him of a fuzzy teddy bear—or a peach. The door at the top of the stairs was open, and the gorgeous, extravagant, heart-warming scent wafted down.

"Howdy, howdy," Charmaine said. "Off to school?"

"Sort of. My first class isn't for a few hours," Rhan said. He tilted his head toward the stairs and grinned, needy and shameless. "Is that coffee?"

The top story of 105 Dalhousie was nothing like the bottom. Hardwood floors gleamed, offset with brightly colored rag rugs. The day was too overcast for sunlight, but every room looked warm, the walls hung with dried floral arrangements, bursts of earthtones in browns and greens and pinks.

In the kitchen the counters were crowded with spices, cannisters and cooking utensils—baking was imminent. Rhan sat down at the maple table and Charmaine set a mug in front of him.

"Slave to the bean?" she said with a wink. "Me, too. I grind every pot fresh."

Rhan was surprised to see the big gray-and-white cat at his feet; he was even more surprised when it jumped suddenly into his lap. It was a strange sensation as the animal began to knead at his thighs, trying to create a more hospitable resting place.

"Hi," Rhan said uncertainly to the cat. "Ow, watch the claws."

Charmaine set a mixing bowl and a cannister of flour on the table. "Hope you're not allergic," she said. "Albert thinks every human is a potential couch."

Eventually the cat curled up and Rhan drank his coffee while Charmaine measured and mixed and asked him about SAIT. He told her the truth, but the edited version, the kind of truth he would have told Gran—what was hard, what he liked, how he'd already had a clip air on a local station.

"Is that what she was so excited about?" Charmaine asked.

Rhan felt the heat in his neck, his cheeks. "Who?"

"The girl who was over the other night," Charmaine said, smiling coyly. "The floor is kind of thin…"

Rhan didn't speak. He was remembering every word, every sound that might have filtered up, especially the bits that weren't family entertainment.

The shock must have shown in his face. Charmaine laughed. "Oh, relax! It's only a certain…pitch that comes through. Besides," she gave him a tap that left a little puff of flour on his shoulder, "you're young. That's what I told Claire-Marie. He's young."

And a fool, Rhan thought. "Where's Claire-Marie?" he said, changing the subject.

Charmaine sprinkled flour onto the table and dropped the dough onto it. She went to work with a rolling pin that made a faint squeak.

"At the university. She's a professor. Head of Women's Studies, actually," she finished proudly.

"Good," Rhan said. "They need to be studied. I hope she publishes the instruction manual."

Charmaine smiled.

"Are you still off work because of your surgery?" Rhan asked.

Charmaine gestured around her with white-dusted hands. "This is my office," she said cheerfully. "I work at home. I'm your friendly neighborhood numerologist."

"I've heard of that," Rhan said. Actually, he'd read about it briefly, in Zoe's books. "It's sort of like astrology?"

"Sort of. But instead of the planets, it works from the premise that all letters have a numerical value, a vibration. Who we are and who we will be resonates in that vibration, through our name. Have you ever been done?" she asked after a moment.

Rhan shook his head.

"I'm not surprised," Charmaine said. "Zoe's more into auras, healing channels and all that." She looked up from the dough, a glint in her eyes. "Do you want me to do you?"

"Will it take long?"

"Well, it can, if I do the whole karma thing, life pinnacles and stuff. I don't have time for that today. But we could do a quickie."

Rhan shrugged. "Sure."

Charmaine went to the sink and washed her hands. She looked excited. "I've been itching to do you," she admitted, "but I couldn't without your birth date and middle name."

"I don't have a middle name," Rhan said.

Charmaine was wiping her hands on a tea towel but she stopped cold. "Really?"

"Is that a problem?"

Charmaine seemed to be thinking. "No. It's just...odd. Are you absolutely sure?"

"I've got my birth certificate," Rhan said, reaching for his wallet. Albert was unsettled and jumped off his lap, indignant. Charmaine took the card and gathered a pencil and paper. Rhan's side of the table was undusted by flour so she pulled a chair over beside him. There was something safe and comfortable about being next to her, Rhan thought. She smelled like cinnamon.

Charmaine copied his name onto the paper, then stopped again. "Your birthday is Halloween? That's today."

Rhan straightened, astonished. "Get out! Is it?" What kind of fog had he been in these last few weeks? He'd never forgotten his birthday in his life.

"Odd," Charmaine said again, "especially when you don't believe in coincidence." She began scribbling numbers above and below the letters of his name. It seemed to Rhan as if she was adding them up.

"Now, there are no good or bad numbers," she said as she worked. "Each has positive and negative aspects. What I'm doing for you is a sum total vibration, what we call a Life Expression."

After she'd totaled the number, she paused. Then she did it all again. Then she got up, grinning sheepishly. "Don't laugh. I know it's only seven digits, but I want a calculator."

"Sure," Rhan said. He was still thinking about his birthday, that maybe he should buy himself something, a present.

The number on the calculator came out as it had on the paper: thirty-three.

Charmaine took a breath. "Okay," she said. She explained that normally she would add the numbers up, then reduce the total down to a single digit. Thirty-four, for example, would become seven.

"But there are three numbers we don't reduce— eleven, twenty-two and thirty-three. Those are called Master Numbers, and they denote people who've come into the world with a greater…power," Charmaine said.

The word seemed to thump him on the side of the head. "Is that good?" Rhan asked.

"Well, it can be. Power just means voltage. How it works out is up to the individual. It's just that for Master Numbers, there's no half-way. Good means great. Bad means, well…really bad." She laughed to lighten the silence that had slipped into the room. "I don't mean to get weird on you. It's just rare."

He was suddenly uncomfortable. Master Number sounded like a duty, a bigger concept than he wanted to deal with right now. He had a life to get back to.

"Well, thanks. I'd better get going," Rhan said. He moved to get up but she stopped him with a hand over his. The warmth seemed to go all the way up his arm.

"That pamphlet that was in your pocket when we did the laundry," Charmaine started.

"I threw it out," Rhan blurted. "Somebody just gave it to me." Half true—he would throw it out now. He was embarrassed by what had happened last night. He didn't want anyone to know, especially not this woman who was nice to him.

"Well, be careful," she said kindly. "We're all magnets. Never mind what we want. We have to be careful what we attract."

"Women?" Rhan said hopefully. Charmaine laughed as she walked him to the door. "Well, I hope you get your wish. Have a good birthday, sexy Scorpio." She gave him a teasing little push.

Rhan went down the stairs feeling a lot better

than when he'd come up. He didn't know what to make of it all. He didn't feel like a Master anything. But he was glad it was his birthday. He felt older, just knowing.

The door to Mark's office was open and before Rhan saw him he heard his voice, hushed and tense. Rhan slowed to a stop, hanging back out of sight. He didn't mean to listen but he didn't want to walk in at a bad time. He had enough against him already.

"This is my class, my call," Mark was saying. "Don't interfere."

There was silence; Rhan realized the instructor was on the phone.

"I know all about your 'instinct' theory. Save it, okay? Just do your job and I'll do mine." Silence again. "Okay." The receiver clunked down. "Bitch," Mark said softly.

Definitely a bad time, Rhan thought, but before he could back away, Mark burst out with his jacket on, an unlit cigarette in his mouth. He didn't look surprised to see him.

"Let's do this outside," Mark said, before Rhan had a chance to say anything.

There was a small exit down the hall from the studio. The doors opened onto an expanse of lawn, but there was a short metal railing to lean against. Rhan knew it; all the smokers did. But it was strange to be out here with an instructor.

Daylight softened Mark Boutiniere, or maybe it was the supple deerskin jacket. He was all shades of brown and seemed to belong to another era. The sixties, maybe. Rhan took a breath.

"I'm sorry I took the camera off campus, kept it out overnight. I thought I was doing the right thing. I didn't realize I'd screw somebody else up and... I'm sorry. I'll apologize to them, too."

Mark said nothing.

"It's not Jen's fault," Rhan hurried on. "It was my idea and I wouldn't let her bring it back. I wanted to get the tape to the station."

Still Mark said nothing. Rhan could feel anxiety pulling his armor off piece by piece. He didn't know what else to say.

"I can't fail," he pleaded. "I want to work in this field...it's all I want to do."

"Why?"

Rhan wavered, wondering how to put it. How could he explain the feeling, the unshakable calm and order and excitement like a drunken dream? When he looked through the lens he could almost hear the blood moving through his veins.

"Because it makes sense," Rhan said. "And most things don't."

"Okay," Mark said quietly. "That's something. It's hopeful."

Hopeful? Rhan wondered.

"I have no doubt you'll work in camera," Mark continued. "You put the BetaCam on your shoulder and it looks like part of your body. And as a teacher, all the bells go off, because you don't see it very often. All you want to do is rush over and start working with that person and forget everything else."

Rhan didn't believe it. Mark had never rushed over to him. He couldn't remember the instructor helping him at all. He'd sent Jen in to help him edit the cyclist tape. Rhan had gotten the same module, the same information as everyone else but then he'd been left alone to figure it out. He suddenly realized it was on purpose, and he felt cheated.

"Why do you hate me?" Rhan said.

Mark sighed. "I don't hate you. I don't even know you…"

"I know. But no matter what I do it's not good enough," Rhan said.

"Good enough? I've never given a 3.8 on a first shoot in my life!"

"I got airtime, major market airtime," Rhan continued, gathering steam, "and you treat it like it's nothing. I…I thought it was good."

Mark dropped his cigarette and crushed it under his shoe. "What word do you want me to use? *Wunderkind?* Prodigy? If that makes you happy, I'll say it. As for airtime, it's more important than you know. And that's why I'm being such a prick about it."

Rhan was reeling. *Wunderkind?* Where had he heard that before?

"The problem with prodigies," Mark continued, "is that people rush in—to protect them, encourage them, take advantage of them. You could be five or twenty, but it's too young. These people become their own universe. Everything is me, me, me! They lose connection with the world, if they ever had it.

"If a prodigy plays the piano, so what? If it's sports, he usually makes so much money he self-destructs. But TV—camera—that's the most powerful thing in the world. There's the potential to reach people, a lot of people."

Rhan was silent. He'd never thought about the camera that way. He'd only thought about what he could do, not who he would reach.

"Talent isn't wisdom, Rhan," Mark said quietly. "I know because I've seen it before. Yeah, I'm hard on you. I'm going to be harder. The assignment is still an F. But if you want to show me something, show me you're professional enough to come back to class anyway."

Rhan felt the news settle on his shoulders like snow. Still an F. But he wanted Single Camera Production, and he wanted it with Mark Boutiniere. He didn't know if he liked him, but he wanted to keep watching him.

"Okay," Rhan said.

Mark finally smiled. "Okay."

Back in the building, classes had just changed. The hallway was busy and full of people. Mark was hurrying and Rhan kept up to him, not walking together but traveling in the same direction. Rhan heard his name the same moment he smelled the perfume.

He'd forgotten what she looked like. For a split second he just stared, captivated by the gold-dusted look of her in a hallway crowded with sweatshirts and jeans.

"I saw your clip on 2," Marlene said breathlessly. "It was fabulous, just a ringer."

"You saw it?" Rhan asked, amazed.

"I think everybody saw it," Marlene said. She glanced beyond him, over his shoulder. Rhan realized Mark had stopped, too.

"I think it's the best piece of tape to come out of first year," Marlene said defiantly, her eyes on Mark. Rhan felt the praise like a starburst.

"Thanks!"

She looked back at him and smiled, a quick flash of summer. She gave his arm a friendly squeeze.

"We'll talk sometime," Marlene said, and she slipped into the crowd. Rhan wasn't sure he felt the ground under his feet for the rest of the afternoon.

TWELVE

RADIO CTSR was broadcast from a control booth on the second floor of H Building, next to the audio labs. The second year Audio and Broadcast News students ran it, afternoons and most evenings. It was a genuine but weak transmission with a signal that could be picked up within a few blocks of the campus, running with news broadcasts and commercials. Protocol was strict. Bill Robertson regularly reviewed the air tapes as part of the Second Years' marks, and he seemed to listen to every shift—beyond human capability.

"If God stops listening, Gold 'n' Gravel is still listening," the Second Years lamented.

When his classes were over, Rhan found himself in the control booth with Devon McGuinness for the four to five o'clock shift. It was absolutely forbidden, of course, "but give the man a thrill on his *birthday*," Devon said.

It was fun, even though Devon made him sit on a table because the one chair in the room needed oiling. "That man could hear a squeak in a coma," he explained.

Devon didn't use a chair himself. He did the whole shift standing, when he was still, which wasn't often. The second the microphone was off, he was a whirlwind—pulling music CDs, commercial carts, prerecorded sound effects.

The station playlist wasn't current but it wasn't bad, yet Rhan soon learned that Devon loved what every On-Air loved: the sound of his own voice.

"The devil didn't come down from Georgia, boys and girls. He came from County Cork and he is *among* you!" Sound effect—chilling scream. "Just another afternoon in paradise with Devon bad-to-worse-to-wicked McGuinness on C...T...S...R!"

Devon loved live ads and promos. He kept pounding the Great SAIT Nightmare on 16th Avenue, the Halloween party scheduled for that night in the students' recreation center. Off air, he badgered Rhan to go, who argued that he didn't have a costume, or a date. Dev grabbed a cart off the sound-effects rack and slipped it into the machine. Violins.

"I've just heard a sad story. There is a man—young, healthy, fully operational—who will *not* be attending the infamous Nightmare on 16th Avenue because frankly, ladies, you haven't done your bit..."

Rhan was waving wildly, panicked.

"This is a highly *eligible* specimen, ladies, not the layabout you might imagine, a rising star in Communications whose work has already appeared on local television. If one kind soul of the female persuasion would just phone up and give our man a bit of encouragement, I'm sure he would put in an appearance. No names, let's just call him Rocket Man, because it's been such a long, long time..."

Music up—the Elton John classic.

"I'll kill you!"

Devon was cringing and laughing in the corner of the booth. "You can't—it's my show."

Just then, the phone line on the control board lit up. Devon gestured at it triumphantly and hit his reel machine to record—phone calls never went live.

"Yes, caller, you're on the air."

"Yeah," the gruff voice said, "can I get a song…"

"No!"

Devon snapped the call off and rewound the tape.

"I'm walking out that door, Dev," Rhan said.

"Relax! Nobody knows it's you. This is brilliant, man."

Then three things happened at once. The song ended, the phone lit up, and Bill Robertson appeared in the glass window of the door. Flustered, Devon hit the microphone, not the tape.

"Y-yes, caller?"

"Don't put this on the air," the girl said, "but tell the Rocket Man to grow up and stop feeling sorry for himself. He should put on his runners and go to the dance."

"Runners?" Devon said.

Dial tone.

Devon glanced at Gold 'n' Gravel, a face of stone through the glass. "Thank you, caller, for that compassionate response! Compassion," he contin-

131

ued helplessly, "is the noblest of virtues!"

Music up, mike off, Rhan out. But he was barely at the end of the hall when Devon caught up, grinning ruefully as he wiped at his forehead.

"Ah, he loves me like a son," the Irishman said.

"But he'd shoot you like a dog," Rhan said.

"Like a dog," Devon agreed.

Rhan decided to attend Nightmare on 16th Avenue. The phone line was distorted. He didn't know if it had been Jen or not, but in his heart he hoped so. Yesterday, walking out of Mark's office, he'd been so mad and hurt. But after last night, the people he liked seemed more valuable, more rare. And he remembered the secret she'd told him in the car two days ago, how desperate she was not to fail the course. He'd been pretty desperate himself, this afternoon with Mark.

At seven o'clock he was on the eighth floor of residence, knocking at Devon's door. Zorro answered, complete with mask, hat and flowing satin cape. He shook his head at Rhan's street clothes.

"Honestly, how you embarrass me! The least you could do is put on some tights…!"

They stopped on the sixth floor. Devon said they had to pick up Shona and her friends. But as soon as the apartment door opened, he pushed Rhan in first.

"Makeover, ladies!"

They shrieked with fiendish delight.

There was a time, Rhan thought, for honorable surrender. To be surrounded by women in skin-clenching costumes, who trailed perfume as they patted and pawed over him, well, that was a pretty good time.

"I only do cats," the cat-girl with the face paint said.

"Do you take a curl?" Shona the vampire said, tugging the band out of his ponytail and running her fingers through his hair.

"How should I know?" Rhan laughed.

Devon was sitting on the counter and he reached into a drawer and pulled out the aluminum foil.

"Do something NASA," he said. "There's a hot-to-trot young lady looking for a Rocket Man."

They created the helmet out of foil, layer after layer mashed down to fit the shape of his head and neck. It wasn't absolutely form-fitting, but he had to turn his whole body to look left or right. They left the face open and at the last minute the cat-girl decided she could compromise herself artistically, and she painted a wide blue streak across his eyes, a visor.

When they led him to the mirror and his image glinted back at him, startling silver and blue, Rhan caught his breath.

"I don't know if Miss Hot-to-Trot will recognize him," Shona's other friend, a French maid, said doubtfully. "He looks more like a knight."

Rhan thought he was finished, but once the five

of them passed through the front doors of Res into the cool October night, bad-to-worse-to-wicked McGuinness tugged him aside, tugged him right out of his jacket.

Rhan heard an unmistakable rattle.

"Dev—no!"

"Don't be a baby," the Irishman said, shaking up the spray paint. "It's supposed to wash out."

The silver took to his clothes really well, to his hands even better. Rhan was surprised that he allowed it, but then he wasn't the kind of guy who'd let three women wrap his head in tin foil, either. The cat-girl slipped one arm through Rhan's and the other through Shona's, who was already linked to Devon and the French maid. They were five across all the way to the student rec center, walking fast, talking loud. Other people had to scramble out of their way.

The magic caught him by surprise—a six-year-old's magic, but it still worked. He could feel himself growing larger in that silver and blue costume. He couldn't fight the rush of exhilaration and memory. He'd forgotten how much fun this was, alchemy that worked in spite of you. And he decided that just for tonight he'd allow himself to enjoy it. No questions, no judgments, no wrangles with the Universe. He was just going to *be*. That was his birthday present to himself.

The dance was held in the rec center's small gym, but Rhan entered the flashing, pulsing carnival and felt as though he'd walked into one of the gory comics Gran had never let him buy. Loosely based on a castle dungeon, Nightmare on 16th Avenue had been created in the eighties, when there was still a budget for promotion and the most brilliant ACA students could be hired in exchange for beer. Now the displays were showing signs of wear—the torso on the rack was down to a single arm—but there was still lots of ghoulish atmosphere left. A huge leatherette bat swung from an overhead cord, an ideal target.

But the most overwhelming feature was the arched gateway at the end of the room. Almost two stories high, a construction of pipe and gray styrofoam blocks, it looked like a castle's stone entrance, with bars running down through the center. It was secured to the wall but a bleak landscape had been painted behind it—for all the world it seemed that they were inside, looking out. Where did they store this stuff during the rest of the year? Rhan wondered.

"Fetching, isn't it?" Devon called over the throbbing music. The room was packed, a moving throng of dancers and restless spirits who hemmed them in on all sides. "Let's find the table."

CTSR had commandeered two tables along the right wall, and in a room full of bright and wild, they were the brightest. It wasn't just the costumes, it was the intensity of color, the volume of pride, Rhan thought. Their Elvises had the *bluest* suede shoes.

From the time he walked up, Rhan was the man of the moment. He hadn't realized it, but news of his aired freelance tape on Channel 2 had spread through the group like a brush fire. Only a few had actually seen the clip but it didn't matter. A First Year making airtime? It was a miracle! Rhan had to tell the story over and over, and he didn't mind a bit. For the first two hours he drank free beer—celebrating his clip, his birthday, his costume, even though nobody knew what he was supposed to be. Zorro was crushed.

"You poxy lot! He's a Rocket Man. Doesn't anyone listen to my show?"

The table only laughed. Rhan bought him a beer.

He was drinking too fast and he knew it. There were four big plastic cups in front of him, all of them empty. He could feel the alcohol humming through him in a happy glow, but it was nothing like the embrace of the table. People changed seats like musical chairs and it didn't matter—they were all in the same group. In the back of his mind a thought fluttered that he'd come here looking for someone, but in the excited blur of the moment it didn't seem important.

Then, a few familiar notes rolled out over the crowd. The cry went up: "Come on, come on!" Both tables scrambled to the dance floor. Rhan tore off his tin-foil helmet and left it behind—it was too hot anyway.

They rushed onto the floor, a stampede of sixty. The other dancers backed away, intimidated. Rhan caught the arms of the two people closest to him, not caring who they were, because all that mattered was making the Circle.

We are the ones...points of light...

Rhan felt the surge in his chest. These were his friends and this was his country. They had a song and he knew the words. He was singing his heart out.

We blazed the trail...burning all night...

Love like an ocean and he was floating in it, swimming in it, but held safe by an arm on either side. They were linked together, backs to the world, riding wave after wave. Forget beer, Rhan thought. Forget coffee and cigarettes and all his other petty addictions. This was the hit, the fix.

And if our gaze should burn you...keep you awake at night...remember that you asked for love...from the points of light!

They cheered and clapped and stomped on the floor until the huge dungeon gate rattled. Around the gymnasium people were staring—some curious, some hostile. But tonight he had one foot in the Magic Nation and they couldn't touch him. In the glorious noise there was his own defiant yell.

He was halfway back to the table when a cowboy slipped an arm through his. He turned, more surprised than defensive.

"You still owe me a drink," the cowboy said.

Never mind the mustache, he knew those eyes. Her hair had to be tucked up under the Stetson hat. In an oversized shirt and vest, with real rawhide chaps, no wonder he'd missed her at a distance. But he couldn't take his eyes away now.

Jen gestured at the table. "Everybody's talking about the tape. I'm happy for you. God, it's a big deal."

"It's a big deal for you, too," Rhan reminded her. "It was your interview."

"Even if it was only one sentence," Jen said, but she smiled.

They were still walking, but slowly. Rhan wished he knew if she had been the caller. It made a difference, somehow, whether this was an accident, or arranged.

"I know you think I let you down and I probably did," Jen blurted. "But...I can't fail. I really want to work in media. It's all I want to do. I can't fail."

He'd said those same words to Mark. He knew what they meant. It wasn't about a job. It was about a place.

"So I guess you're still really mad," Jen said.

It was hard to be mad at somebody you understood, Rhan thought. And it was impossible to be next to her, even as a cowboy, and not want to touch her.

Rhan stuck out his foot. "I wore my runners."

She laughed and her eyes twinkled under the

brim of the big hat. "Somebody listens to Dev's show," she said.

So she *had* arranged this. Another birthday present. He let his hand slip down to catch hers. He was surprised by how hard she squeezed back.

When they reached the table, Rhan saw that his tin-foil helmet had been taken for a trophy and mounted on a plastic ax at the end of the table. Two more beers had appeared in front of his chair and he gave one to Jen. It went down so quickly he bought another.

CTSR was disintegrating, melting in the liquor and heat. Stage make-up ran and rubbed off, costumes de-constructed and littered the table like body parts on a battlefield. Rhan had to keep blinking to hold the world in focus. The night was sliding, moments of stark clarity that dissolved into a swimming blur of color and sensation. He was acutely aware of Jen's knee pressing against his under the table, and the skeleton sitting at the end of the row, next to his helmet.

A full latex mask covered the man's whole head, a startling contrast of white bone and black hollows. The rest of the costume was simply a black tracksuit; in the dim light the head seemed to float, unattached. It was eerie and fascinating. Rhan couldn't remember seeing the skeleton before. He was ready to go over and see who it was when he felt Jen's hand on the back of his head.

He turned to her. She was stroking his hair, running her fingers through it, entranced.

"It's beautiful," she said. She pulled off her hat and her own hair fell over her shoulders, the same length, the same color as his own.

"Did you notice that we're a set?" she whispered. Rhan reached up and peeled her mustache off gently.

Across the table, Zorro was in another country. His mask dangled around his neck and his hat was tilted perilously. His accent had become thicker with every drink.

"You're a woeful sight, Devon McGuinness," he said to no one. "I'm shocked you see fit to come into a Christian house in that condition…"

Kissing her. He couldn't hear the music anymore, he could only feel it, a steady thump of drums through the floorboards and into him. Her hand on his bare neck under his hair, holding him tight. Deeper and deeper. Raw guitar like metal tearing, crying, breaking away. The sky was falling…

"…to stand in His sight, the maker of miracles. Now you'll get down on your knees in front of the Sacred Heart…"

Get up! Stand up, RanVan.

Rhan pulled himself away, gasping, movement that made the room pitch. Who'd said that?

The skeleton was standing, looking at him out of black sockets.

"Get up!"

The blurred night pulled into sharp and sudden

focus, blue lightning lifted him out of his chair. The sky was falling and he was sober. He went right over the table, cups spinning, spraying beer. He charged onto the crowded dance floor, following the path that the skeleton made as he shoved people out of the way.

But now they all knew, now they were screaming, stumbling into one another as the dungeon gate tore from its wall moorings, coming down. The whole Universe seemed to be traveling through the knight's veins, but the skeleton was faster, fast enough to make it to the far side of the arch.

They caught it at forty-five degrees. RanVan could not feel his arms above his head, holding up the pipe and styrofoam that he knew must weigh hundreds and hundreds of pounds. He felt suspended in a beam of energy. But the arch was dangerously unbalanced, top-heavy from the angle. They could not push it back up. Seconds seemed like hours as they held it while terrified dancers scrambled out from under the bars that would have crushed them.

Finally he looked across at the skeleton.

"Now!" he screamed. In the same second they shoved off and stepped away and the gate came down with a muffled boom that shook the floor.

Around him there was the swirl of noise and horror at what had nearly happened. Shockwaves sent people scurrying, even though the danger was over. The Nightmare on 16th Avenue had come to pass and the room was in motion. Rhan couldn't see his table, his group.

The night hit him suddenly, a boomerang blow of alcohol that told him he should have stopped the party hours ago. He sat down heavily on one of the styrofoam blocks, gulping air. The Master Number was not going to be able to walk by himself.

A blur of black and white. Death's head.

"I need your help," the skeleton said in a low, urgent voice.

"I'm pissed," Rhan said helplessly.

The skeleton pulled him to his feet. With a single expert turn, he draped Rhan's arm over his shoulder and half carried him through the crowd and out of the building.

THIRTEEN

THE cold night air was a welcome shock against Rhan's face and chest. But the campus was rolling, a sickening pitch he could feel in his stomach. He had a terrible certainty about what was going to happen. People were leaving the rec center, milling on the pavement. This was going to be embarrassing.

"Get me somewhere," he mumbled.

The skeleton dragged him around to the secluded side of the building where a sloped hill led to the parking lot below. Rhan tore himself away just in time and, leaning against the back brick wall of the center, he was wretchedly sick. At a respectful distance, the skeleton peeled off the latex mask. Rhan did not have to see. He'd known it was the Iceman from the moment he'd heard the voice in his head. He hated this, the mortal humiliation, weakness in front of this man, but he couldn't stop it. This was not an intellectual process.

At last he stepped away, gasping, swearing. His stomach was better but the rest of the liquor was still in his blood. He felt shaky and dizzy; more defenseless than he wanted to be. Only time would help.

Lee Dahl was wiping the sweat off his face with his forearm—the mask must have been excruciatingly hot. The moisture left in his short hair caught in the moonlight, a sheen.

"What a rush!" he said.

Rhan took an uncertain step, curious in spite of himself.

"Is that how...the power works for you?" he said.

"No, that was my first rescue. I have other talents." Lee was looking at his hands. "That was a *rush*," he said again softly.

"How did you know?" Rhan said.

Lee was surprised. "You told me. I heard you say, Iceman, the sky is falling."

"No, you told *me*! You said to get up."

Lee grinned, wicked and sharp. "This chiller-thriller moment is brought to you by God Himself. Love the effects."

Rhan hesitated. He wanted to ask if Lee believed in God, or what he believed in these days, when he remembered he was talking to scum. Beyond the rec center people were trailing down the grassy slope to their cars. Rhan could hear their voices and it made him brave. The Iceman was in his territory now.

"I'm going back inside and you're not. I don't ever want to see your face."

He started slowly along the wall, one hand on the brick to steady himself.

Lee stepped suddenly in front of him, against the wall.

"I wasn't kidding. I need help."

"Then ask your Nazi friends!"

He hadn't meant to shout but he was mad. Heads turned, a few people slowed their descent.

With a single strong hand, Lee pinned his shoulder to the wall, an abrupt reminder of who was drunk and who wasn't.

"Shut up. This isn't a joke. I'm not safe here."

"No shit!"

"This is about somebody's life, RanVan," Lee said.

To hear his name, so private and personal, was like a hand against his bare skin. This was somebody who knew him and his secrets.

"Hey, do you need some help?"

The Iceman let go; they both turned. A young man had taken a few steps into the shadows with them. His two friends hung back on the path, but close enough. They weren't in costume. The logos on their jackets said Engineering.

The engineer was talking to Rhan, but he was looking at Lee. The Iceman turned aside, pulled back deeper into shadow, but Rhan could feel the warning coming off him like raw electricity. He would fight his way out of this and it would not be nice. And at the same time Rhan was wondering whose life Lee had meant.

"It's okay," he said finally.

For a second the engineer didn't move. He was peering hard at Lee.

"You sure?"

"Yeah. Just…fooling around," Rhan said.

"Okay," the engineer said, backing off. "No offense, man."

The three continued on their way, but talking in low voices.

"I'll tell you everything but I won't tell you here," the Iceman said. "This campus is notorious for anti-skin skins."

Rhan's mind was in the rec center. "I have a date."

"And this is somebody's *life*," Lee said again. "Do you think I would be here for a minute if I didn't have to?"

No. Rhan could see that much in his liquid eyes.

"Besides, if she's worth it, she'll be there tomorrow," Lee continued. He tilted his head down the slope. "My car's in the lot. Can you make it?"

Rhan pushed past him, insulted. It was slow going. He almost fell more than once, but he made it to the parking lot on his own. He was looking for Lee's old car, the white Camaro with personalized licence plate, but approaching a hunter-green Bonneville, Lee pulled out a tiny remote on a keychain. The security system beeped as it disarmed and the doors unlocked with a demure click.

Rhan stared. This car was half the price of a house and it looked it—a dark-green whisper in the night. He thought of the jar stuffed with donations, but this was a different kind of money. You couldn't buy this car five and ten dollars at a time.

"This makes me sick!" he blurted.

Lee opened the driver's side but paused, looking over Rhan's silver spraypainted clothes. "Is that stuff going to come off on the seats?"

Rhan yanked open his side defiantly. "Probably!"

Lee started the engine. Rhan was slapping his pockets—no jacket. Damn! He'd left everything at the table.

"I want a cigarette," he said.

"I don't smoke."

"Then get some!"

"Yes, *sir*." Lee wrenched out of the parking stall in a violent curve. Rhan had to grab the dashboard and his stomach.

The convenience store was a block away. Rhan drummed his fingers, waiting. Half a minute later Lee tossed the package at him as he swung back into the car. Rhan didn't fumble. He knew these deft movements so well—pull the tab, the crackle of cellophane, perfect silver paper tucked in behind the first deck on the left side. The expert snap of a match, then ignition, then better. Breathe in, breathe out. Not all right, but better.

It took him a second to realize they were still at the store, that his silver skin just looked dirty under the fluorescent lights, and that Lee was watching him intently.

"We're all junkies, aren't we?" he said.

"Don't judge me," Rhan shot back.

"I've been in detox four times. I don't judge anybody," the Iceman said.

Four times in three years. Rhan felt the horror press into his skin. That was not a small problem.

But he remembered he wasn't here to feel sorry.

"Just drive," Rhan said. "You've got twenty minutes. Start at the beginning. What are you doing with these...nutcases? Don't tell me you believe this crap!"

The True North was started in Toronto by former lawyer Jim Rusk, as a monitoring group for Canada's immigration practices.

"He said he got sick of prosecuting F.O.B's... fresh off the boat," Lee explained. The True North tried to monitor how many people were granted status, where they were from, how much money was spent on them, and what percentage became a "criminal element."

"Did you check the records of your own membership?" Rhan snapped.

Lee ignored him. At first he was one of the "foot soldiers." Their role was to be visible and vocal, he explained. If there was a demonstration, they'd put on a show. The people under twenty-five usually chanted about unemployment, and how there weren't enough jobs for the people who'd been born here, never mind newcomers. Lee made the news more than once.

"I do a great angry young man," he said, a gleam in his eyes. "You'd swear I really was looking for work."

About twenty, mostly men, had lived in Jim's big house like a dorm. Once, an anonymous benefactor flew them all to Ottawa, to yell at the House of Commons.

148

"I partied for two days. We ran into a group of straight edge guys. They're anti-racist, anti-everything. You can always pick them out because they paint black X's on their hands. We had some great fights."

That's when the True North also began to attract skinheads—true white purists who screamed and fought and schemed for real. Lee shook his head and sighed. As membership began to grow, in numbers and across the provinces, the True North became more organized. Jim Rusk had money and he had a talent for getting more. He began dreaming of himself as a leader, not really as a political party, but as a grass-roots movement.

Rhan was getting frustrated. Lee wasn't telling him anything important.

"But why? Why them in the first place?"

The Iceman glanced across the seat at him. Streetlight over the windshield lit him up even paler than he was.

"Because they took me," he said.

"What a stupid reason!"

"Is it?" Lee shot back. "Tell me, *knight*, that you've had a good life. Tell me that the power makes people love you, that you're surrounded by family and friends, that you're happy with your place in *society*."

A bolt of painful memory, rounding a dark corner into a blast of hate, cringing on the ground while people he knew looked on. But he didn't have to tell Lee about the vengeance of Reine Dahl.

"What happened when you moved to Toronto to live with your dad?" Rhan said quietly.

Lee took a long breath and let it out slowly. "You know, he never came to see me in detox, not once, not even to say, Hey, are you alive? Jim came every day."

They were nearing downtown. The car interior was brighter from the streetlights.

"So, it was…kinda fun. Think about it," Lee continued. "Dress up and play bad guy. Every night is Halloween." He grinned. "You walk shoulder to shoulder down a sidewalk and people cross the street."

Instant replay—Zorro and the cat and the vampire and the Rocket Man, linked up and bold, pedestrians scrambling out of their way. Rhan felt his stomach tighten. This was not far enough away from him. He lit another cigarette.

"So that's worth beating people for?" he said.

"I don't beat anybody. I have other talents."

"Like what?"

Espionage had become important in the last few years. With anti-fascist groups springing up, and squabbling between factions, a lot of time was spent gathering information—who knew what about whom, where they would be and what they would do. And that's when the Iceman stopped being a foot soldier.

"I know where to look," Lee said. "I guess and I

guess right. There was a raid, before we left Toronto. Fire bomb—amateur stuff but it would have been bad. Except they raided an empty house. Jim trusts me now."

The alcohol warmth was wearing off. Rhan felt a chill crawl over him.

"So that's how the power works for you," he said bitterly. "That's what you do with it. Protect violent men from other violent men."

"Aren't you *noble*, Mr. Media." Lee bit the words. "I sat at that table, I heard about your fire. I'm so impressed. What a hero."

The strike hurt. Rhan used to believe in heroes.

"I've met enough media," Lee continued grimly. "You should look at your own people sometime, listen to them, how excited they get by disaster. Even if they have to create it. Fucking vampires."

A year ago the True North relocated its base to Calgary. Lee believed that a lot of the money came from Alberta and anyway, Jim wanted to rub shoulders with grass-roots politicians. There was a lot happening in the province—Christian Patriots, skinheads, but also the extreme right-wing business sector that Jim was so good with. Rhan thought of the tanned face in the hallway, the campaign handshake. He wondered if the man even saw the swastikas among the business suits.

"There's even an Alliance," Lee said, "but the game is changing…"

"Phantom cells," Rhan cut in impatiently. Lee was surprised.

"Yeah, cells. Leaderless resistance. Except Jim is somebody who only ever wanted to be a leader."

Rhan was getting tired of hearing about Jim Rusk, and the endless circling around the real reason he was in the car.

"So he's going to kill somebody?" he demanded.

Lee looked at him, his eyes like cold bits of glass. "No. Never. It's one of the cells."

"Who are they after?"

"I don't know."

"Then who...?"

"I don't know! There was a big inquiry a couple of years ago, prosecutions. Some people went to jail. It might be connected to that," Lee said vaguely. His voice hardened. "All I'm sure of is that it's somebody really important."

They were almost back at the campus. Lee pulled into the convenience store parking lot, only at the edge this time, out of the light. The Bonneville's engine was a barely audible hum.

"How are you sure?" Rhan said.

"I'm dreaming it," Lee said. "Over and over. There's a fortress, the whole thing just for one man. I can't see his face, but I know he's important, like a king. This wild...army comes through the wall, I don't even know how..."

Because it's melting, Rhan thought with a pang. Because it's only ice.

"Where are you when this happens?" he interrupted.

"Nowhere. I'm only watching, I'm not in it."

"This army," Rhan said quietly. "Could they be Vikings?"

Lee looked at him, intent and piercing. "What do you know? What did you see?!"

"Just tell me! Why would they be Vikings?"

"Norse mythology is the skinhead theme song," Lee said, a slight, hard smile on his face. "In their minds, they are Vikings."

Now Rhan was scared. Now this seemed real, and close. Too close. He was understanding and he didn't want to. He twisted around in his seat.

"You go to the cops, Lee. You go *tonight*. You name every name, you describe every face…"

"Then Jim's a dead man."

"Why?"

"Because I think he knows something. He's getting calls, late. He's trying to talk somebody out of something." Lee sighed. "He doesn't know he's not their leader," he said to himself.

"Then Jim Rusk has a problem. But I shouldn't even be in this car."

Rhan scooped the cigarettes off the dash and grabbed the door handle. Lee caught his shirt.

"Come and see…what you see. That's all I want. I need more information. Then maybe we can figure out a way…"

"No!" Rhan broke the hold. "This isn't my

problem. It's over my head and it's over yours. You go to the cops and get out of this now."

"I won't leave," the Iceman said simply.

"Then you're a coward, and you're as guilty as they are. And I'm sorry I saved you."

He threw his shoulder against the door and burst out, slamming it behind him. He started walking, not fast, because he felt a sudden, unsteady wave now that he was on his feet. The cold seemed to seize him; he hadn't noticed it before. In a few steps he was shivering.

"There's somebody...who won't leave," Lee called.

Rhan turned. The Iceman was out of the car, standing with the door open. In the dim light his face seemed to hover above the car's dark, shiny roof.

Rhan's mind flitted back to the crowded room, the two close-cropped, hobnail girls, so much alike that he could only remember one face.

"Then she's as stupid as you are," he called back. The cold was shaking his voice. "You deserve each other! And it's still not my problem."

"Yes, it is," Lee said. "Because now you know."

The truth seemed to hit Rhan in the chest.

"It doesn't make me care," he called boldly.

Lee got back in the car. But on the way to the exit he paused, window open. Rhan took a step back. He didn't want this man to see him trembling.

"Do you ever check your pulse to make sure you

have a heart?" the Iceman said, an edge to his voice. He thrust a jacket out the window at him. Rhan was surprised but he caught it, his arms full of soft, smooth leather.

"My cell phone number's in the pocket," Lee said. "The clock's running, RanVan."

FOURTEEN

I T'S not the fall that kills you, Gran had always
said. It's the sudden stop.

Friday morning, November 1, at 7:30 A.M.,
Rhan understood exactly what she meant.

"Wow," the convenience store clerk said. "That
must have been some party."

"Aspirin, please," Rhan whispered. The clerk
pulled the small container off a display but it never
hit the counter. Rhan opened it where he stood and
downed two pills with the scalding coffee he already
had in his other hand.

"You should call in sick," the clerk said sympa-
thetically.

"I'm still standing," Rhan said, handing over the
money. But when he caught his reflection in the
rounded security mirror, he wondered why.

Sick was a pale word for it. He'd had a shower
this morning but it seemed that the blue tint clung
stubbornly around his eyes, just enough to give him
the hollows of dead man. And he hadn't shaved. He
barely had the co-ordination to hold a toothbrush.
He didn't dare put a razor to his throat. If this
morning had been any class other than Television
Production, he would still be in bed.

"Have a nice day," the clerk said.

Rhan couldn't come up with any response that
wasn't profane, so he said nothing.

Two steps out of the door, he lit up.

We're all junkies, aren't we?

Go away, Rhan told the ghost as he shook out the match. I can't think about you today.

But he was still wearing Lee's jacket. The black leather was deep and rich and heavy on his back. Too heavy. He felt as if he was holding up the whole night with his shoulders.

His first instinct was to go to the police, to tumble this horror into someone else's lap. But what would he say? I've heard there's going to be a murder. I don't know who or when, but I'm having visions of Vikings so that makes it true? And what if Lee was right, that Jim Rusk knew enough to be suspect if there was a sudden investigation? The man might be scum but Rhan knew he couldn't let him take the blame for an information leak. Lee was counting on that.

"I hate you," he said out loud, and the words were a soft puff of frost in the cold morning air. He hated the sad, violent life he knew too much about. He hated the addictive personality, the lonely, shameless need for people—for a group, and the adoration he could hear every time Lee said Jim Rusk's name. What was this, a father fixation? Well, he hated it.

Do you ever check your pulse...?

Don't talk to me about my heart, Rhan thought savagely. You're the one running with fascists. Maybe you haven't dumped anybody in the river but you know people who have. No job, no skills, but a fifty-thousand-dollar car and a private line. Don't talk to me about *vampires*.

He rounded the corner and stopped. They'd changed the poster at The Odyssey and a new brilliance filled the front window, red and blue and yellow. The real heroes were always in primary colors. Rhan stood, riveted by the towering image of that other man without a planet.

He'd had one minute last night that was set apart from everything else, one electric-blue moment when he'd done the right thing. He remembered going over the table, the whoosh that had carried him through the crowd. He remembered the weightless, timeless sensation of holding up the wall, like being a wire that carried an electric current. But most of all he remembered the other feeling, huge and humbling—what it was like to help people. It had been a long time.

As he started away he touched Superman's foot through the glass; he didn't even know why.

By the time he reached H Building, the aspirin had blunted the roughest edge of pain. Rhan was nervously shuffling lies like cards in his head. He knew he'd have some explaining to do—what had happened and where he'd gone. For most people he could make something up, but he didn't know what he was going to tell Jen. That he could hear a display come away from its moorings in the middle of a blaring dancehall—in the middle of a kiss? That he liked her so much he'd just left her sitting at the table without a word, and never went back to find her?

Rhan felt suddenly tired. Once you started to care about someone, even little lies seemed heavy.

Mark hadn't arrived yet; the class was waiting in the hallway outside Studio A. Everyone who'd been at the table the night before was moving slowly, looking slightly gray under the fluorescent lights. It struck Rhan that it was the younger students who were in the worst shape. We don't know when to quit, he thought.

He was still the man of the moment. As soon as they saw him, they came up, peppering him with questions. How had he known the wall was going to fall? Who was the guy with him? And then where had he gone?

"You went over that table like...a Rocket Man!" Jeff said excitedly. "Then, ka-boom!"

"Don't shout, Jeff," Kaitlyn said irritably, in pain.

"The place was pandemonium and you were just gone. It was spooky."

Rhan gave the story he'd prepared—that he didn't know the skeleton, but that they'd both seen the wall tear away at the same time. After that, "I thought I should get home while I was still vertical," Rhan said with a grin.

"Without your jacket?" Jen said suddenly, beside him. It was draped over her arm. Rhan stepped aside, leading her away from the group, and took it from her.

"I'm sorry," he said in a low voice.

"We were so worried!" she said. "I thought you'd been abducted. We searched the whole rec center and then we went outside looking for you."

Rhan was touched. He'd never expected people would worry. But he shook his head. "I was just in bad shape."

"It didn't look like it. I've never seen anybody move so fast in my whole life."

Rhan shrugged weakly. "Reflexes," he said.

She looked at him for a moment, brown eyes searching his face. "Do you think I'm stupid?"

"What?" He felt the shock go through him in a swift cramp.

"I was there," Jen said. "Remember? You were kissing me and suddenly you just froze. That isn't a reflex. You didn't see anything—your eyes were closed."

He didn't know what to say, but she wasn't finished.

"And I was at the fire, too," she continued, an edge to her voice. "There was no sound, Rhan, no reason to go off shot. Okay, so I'm not really technical, but I'm *conscious*. I can hear and I can see, and just because I don't call you up on every lie doesn't mean I believe them." She hesitated. "When are you going to like me enough to tell me the truth?"

Rhan's face was burning. He felt naked in front

of Jen and he didn't know if it was terrifying or a relief. But the truth was not a small thing, and he didn't hand it out to strangers. He wanted her to know that. "I only trust people I trust," he said.

Jen straightened. "Oh, sure. Steal my lines," she said, but she looked shaken.

"Well, good morning, my little points of light!" Mark Boutiniere sang out, cheerful and loud, as he strode toward the studio. There was a general groan. "Everybody ready to work, work, work?"

"You're a sadist," Kaitlyn muttered.

"I live for these moments," Mark said, standing at the door as he ushered them in, "because I'm not dumb enough to have them anymore."

Jen looked away but she touched Rhan's arm as she left. The conversation wasn't over, he thought.

The studio god was passing judgment as they filed into the room: the Undead; the Grateful Dead; Miss Demeanor; Missed the Boat. Rhan cringed and tried to hurry past—he already knew what he looked like—but the instructor caught his shoulder in a little shake.

"Glad you could make it," was all he said. It was an unexpected kindness, almost a gift.

It was not set up to be an easy day. They were divided into two teams to tape a simple mini-production: a talk-show format, they had to move from camera one to camera two, back to camera one for the break intro, go to commercial one, commercial two, then back to the show. It would be three minutes of finished tape and they only had an hour to do it.

Rhan was in the first production as switcher, the critical man keying the commands through the main board, switching cameras and tape feed, making sure graphics came up where they were supposed to. The director made the decisions but the switcher controlled what came up on the screen. Rhan loved being switcher—buttons and bars spread out in front of him, the tension of being in the middle of a do-or-die situation. But he'd never thought he'd have to face it with a hangover, or with Bob Arnott at his left elbow as director.

That morning Bob was extremely frustrated with the quality of personnel at his disposal. He argued with the floor director, script assistant and the lighting crew. Rhan sat quietly, grateful for the dim lighting of the control booth, listening to the endless banter on his headset but not saying a word. He rehearsed his dissolves and cuts, checked levels and titles.

"Get me tone and bars," Bob snapped. "Get your levels."

"I did the levels fifteen minutes ago," Rhan said.

"Well, get them again!"

Bitter words sat on Rhan's tongue but they stayed there. He was thinking about the sign in Mark's office, about what a professional was.

Finally Mark came into the booth, shutting the door behind him.

"Come on, already! Your talent has been sitting in that light for ten minutes. They're sweating like pigs. And we've got the second show to do today."

"Everybody's a mess," Bob complained. "I can't get shit out of these people."

Mark flashed him a dark look. He glanced at the monitors. "There's a green gel on the spot. Get rid of it. Green makes people look sick."

Bob barked the message through his headset mike.

"Rhan, check the scope. You've got glare." Rhan scrambled to adjust.

"Kaitlyn, give me a thirty-second count as soon as we're at twelve," Mark gestured at the clock. He leaned forward to talk into the control booth microphone. "People, this is it. Cue the talent and listen for the count."

"Thirty," Kaitlyn broke in, counting down the seconds, "twenty-nine…twenty-eight…"

"Do your show, Bob," Mark said, stepping back, arms folded over his chest. The switcher would have enjoyed the look on the director's face, if he hadn't been panicking himself.

Three minutes flew by when you were taping a show, Rhan discovered, and it crawled when you were showing it to the world. There were lots of mistakes, bad cues and brief delays that looked enormous on the playback monitor. Rhan felt the biggest screw-up belonged to him—a return to camera that should have been the second commercial. But Bob had told him to do it.

"I got mixed up," Bob argued. "He had a script. He should have followed it."

"No," Mark thundered. "You're the director, he's listening to you. His job is give you what you ask for." The room was silent, chastened. Mark looked out at all of them. "You want to cover your ass? Go work for city hall. You want to be a professional? Take responsibility." He looked back to Rhan and nodded. "You did the right thing. Good work."

In that moment, a sick man was almost well.

"Okay," Mark continued. "Let's take a ten-minute break…"

The room dissolved into noisy relief; the lecture was over for the moment. Rhan rifled through the pile of jackets to find the Iceman's black leather—it was warmer than his own and he was going outside. He glanced at Jen but she was nervously checking notes with Jeff. She was on camera one for the second production and he could see the worry on her face across the room. He felt the urge to go over and help—he could handle the metal giants in his sleep—but he held himself back. She'd said she wanted to do it herself.

He pulled on his jacket but stopped paces from the door. Marlene Foye hovered in the open space, like a salesman trying to get a foot in. Mark was blocking her way.

There were some people, Rhan thought, who always made you think of how you looked. Today

Marlene was pink on pink on powder blue, a turtle-neck and blazer over blue jeans—seashell colors. He was suddenly profoundly aware that he hadn't shaved, and that on some guys it looked macho and on him it just looked…unwashed.

"Look, I'm in a meeting at noon. My day is booked. If he's done his shift I don't see why—"

"Marlene," Mark cut her off, not exactly the way Rhan expected professionals to talk to each other.

They both seemed to notice Rhan at the same time.

"Hi," Marlene said, and she smiled. "Do you have a few minutes?"

He looked at Mark, who sighed, beaten. "You're finished for today. We'll be running the second team's show at around 11:30. You should see that."

"Sure," Rhan said, but his mind was in motion. What was going on?

Out in the hallway, he didn't know what to say. He wasn't easily intimidated, and he wasn't espe-cially polite. She just seemed so *bright*, Rhan thought. Was that fame or beauty or what? He didn't know, but somehow it made it hard to speak.

"Great jacket," Marlene said, tugging at his sleeve. "You want a coffee?"

"Sure," Rhan said again, and he cringed. You are not having a monosyllabic conversation, Van, he told himself. This is just a human being. Get over it!

Marlene bought, and she started talking the moment they set down their mugs.

"How are you holding up? I know the first few months are kind of rough." She grinned. "We used to call him Boot-Camp Mark. Did he give you the I-am-your-studio-god speech?"

Rhan was astounded. She had gone here—she had been in Mark's class. It was as if the planet Jupiter had landed in his back yard.

"First day," he said.

"Well, if it's any consolation, he lightens up in second year, just a bit." Her voice lowered. "But I knew he would be especially tough on you because of me."

"You?"

"You didn't have any media background, no references, so…I put my own name down," she said. "I'm sort of your sponsor."

A painful burst of revelation. Mark had been telling the truth that first day. "You're saying they weren't going to let me in," he blurted, the heat rushing to his face. "You're saying I don't deserve to be here!"

Her hand came down suddenly over his wrist.

"I made the selection jury run your tape four times. I thought it was just…electric. To me, raw talent, raw instinct is more important than pre-training." Marlene released her grip. "There are no rules, Rhan, if you're good enough."

He was sitting rapt, drinking the words like a man in the desert.

She seemed to be enjoying his shock. "And

you're proving me right," she said. "I'm sure Willie Shine almost peed himself over that clip, he'd be so excited."

"Is he the one who told you about it?"

She laughed, small and clear; a delighted sound. "That's so cute!" She leaned in on the table. "Do you think there's a minute of airtime in this city that isn't chewed over, chewed through, by every other station? I had to explain to my news director why *we* didn't get it, seeing that I teach here."

"You could have had it," Rhan said hurriedly. "I just went to the closest station…"

She waved the apology away. "Next time. Listen, I'm thrilled to see you do well. You're my vindication. I always have these arguments with people about talent and instinct, that there are some things you *can't* teach. When you succeed, it proves me right." She gave his arm a friendly squeeze. "I love being right."

Her smile was on him like sunlight. It was as if the months of work and worry had been lifted off his shoulders. For the first time it seemed real, that he was good enough.

Marlene took a sip of her coffee, then leaned forward again. "Now, I know you've got a busy day so I won't take up too much of it," she said.

I could sit here for the rest of my life, Rhan thought.

"That man you were talking to outside the rec center last night. Do you know who he is?"

His stomach plummeted. She hadn't been there. How did she know? And how could he lie? This woman had sponsored him.

"I'm not part of any group," he said.

"I didn't say that you were," Marlene answered carefully. They sat in silence that was not a void. Rhan could feel the draw like a magnet, her earnest, intent face telling him that this was real and important. But he remembered the dark back wall of the rec center, engineering students, and the wave of fear coming off the Iceman. That was real, too.

"Well, I know who he is," Marlene said finally. "He's not the one I want. But he's close."

FIFTEEN

THE Iceman picked up on the second ring "Yeah?"

"All right," Rhan said into the receiver. "I'll see what I can do."

"Good." A single word, but he could hear the relief in it.

"I want to be somewhere Jim is," Rhan said. "I want to be in the same room."

"Why?"

"Because I just do. It's a hunch. I don't know how this works," Rhan continued, "but if he's holding all this information, maybe he becomes like a channel?" He was making it up and he didn't sound as certain as he wanted to.

For a moment there was nothing; Rhan could hear the protective caution.

"It's…not going to be easy. He has a full schedule."

"It's Friday night, for Christ's sake. Doesn't the man go out? Have a social life?"

"He's Gandhi," Lee said wearily. "Gandhi never partied."

Gandhi? Rhan thought. "Well, tell him even God took a day off," he argued.

Lee laughed—a surprising sound. Rhan realized he'd never heard it.

"Okay," the Iceman said finally. "I think I can

get him to Club Valhalla." He gave the address; it wasn't listed. "It's not really private," Lee continued. "Pay your cover and they'll probably let you in. But don't look like media and…do something about your hair."

Bitter memory—a knee in his back, iron grip holding his head up. *Give me a knife.*

"If they think you're queer, no one can save you," Lee said, and he hung up.

Rhan laid the receiver back in the cradle. "Club Valhalla," he said.

Marlene pushed off the filing cabinet she had been leaning against. "They play *Oi*," she said. "Hate music. A hardcore place. It'd be fantastic to get footage of him in there."

Rhan had never made it back to Mark's class. They'd been in her small office at SAIT all morning. She had a playback monitor and she'd been showing him rough cuts of tape taken over the summer and on her recent assignment—this was why she'd been away. Rhan had seen lots of demonstrations, lots of yelling, chanting foot soldiers. There were interviews with victims—Jews, Sikhs, Chinese nationalists—whose faces would be blurred, voices altered in the final production, but in this moment they were completely real and close. Rhan sat in silence, story after story pressing him into the chair, soaking into his skin. One man had been beaten so savagely he'd lost an eye and bitten off part of his own tongue. His strained speech was haunting.

"Do you know what it is not to be a person? To look into a face that doesn't see you? That was the most terrible thing."

There was no footage of the True North, and not a soul who'd go on record about money, where it might come from and what it was used for. Like Tory Samuels, Marlene believed there were a few key figures who were the major "arteries" into the system and who funded other groups. She believed Jim Rusk was one of those arteries.

"Two years ago, the man was an interviewing fool—anytime, anywhere. You'd swear he was running for office. Then, suddenly he became unreachable. I don't know what happened."

The Iceman happened, Rhan thought. If Lee's opinion carried any weight with his boss, the media would not get close to Jim Rusk.

She already knew the name, Lee Dahl. He was a "face," someone who was regularly visible as part of Rusk's entourage.

"Part of the inner circle, probably like a lieutenant. These guys are always building little armies," Marlene said with a grim smile.

Rhan hadn't lied to her. He told her he knew Lee from Thunder Bay. But he hadn't told her why they'd been talking behind the rec center. He could feel the tug of war inside him. This was someone's life, but he didn't know enough! If only he had more—a name, a place—he was sure Marlene would know who to tell. He could let go of this weight that seemed to grow larger and heavier by the minute.

Marlene unlocked a cupboard and took out a case, half the size of a box of chocolates. Inside was the smallest, most slender piece of video equipment Rhan ever seen. It was barely as big as his hand.

"Camcorder?" he said in disbelief.

"Featherweight, ultra-sensitive in low light, the sound field is unbelievable," Marlene said, touching it in wonder. "Vic Ducharme got footage in Saudi Arabia with this." She looked up at Rhan again. "There's a big rally on Saturday and Jim Rusk will be there, but I've got lots of rallies, lots of podium speeches. I know you can get me something else."

He'd known it was coming to this and yet when he took the piece of slim, cool metal in his hands, he was suddenly scared. The images from the tapes were still raw in his memory. What was he walking into? He was just one guy. What could he get that would make a difference? How could he be sure he was doing the right thing?

Marlene was watching him.

"All you have to do is tell the truth," she said quietly. "You don't have to carry it, just tell it. Let the world deal with it."

The words slid over him, silvery and smooth, a relief. Wasn't telling the truth always the right thing?

She handed him the case, and the little leather

holster that would let him carry the camera under his jacket, unseen, until he had to use it.

"You're going to have an exciting career," Marlene said. She gave his shoulder an encouraging squeeze. "Just get me something to hang him with."

◆

Rhan pulled into the Club Valhalla parking lot that night at 9:15. He'd seen in a glance that the lot was full, but he drove up and down the aisles, looking for the green Bonneville. When he didn't see it, he decided to check the nearby side streets. He wasn't going in unless his target was there.

A block and a half from the club, the glimmer of hunter green caught his eye and kicked his heart to the next level. This was a go. There were lots of spaces on the quiet office street, but Rhan pulled far ahead before he parked. No one knew his car and he wanted to keep it that way.

He got out and glanced around, but there wasn't even traffic. He pulled off his jacket and slung the loop of the holster over his left shoulder. The other end clipped behind him on his back belt loop. Out of its case, the little camera fit snugly into the pocket that hung against his ribs, a distinct nudge every time he moved. He could have it out and filming in under three seconds. He knew because he'd practiced at home.

He pulled on Lee's leather jacket again with a pang of regret. He'd have to give it back sometime and he was starting to like it. Tonight he thought it made him look more intimidating and he needed it to. He didn't want anyone to approach him. The rest of the outfit was to keep him from being recognized: black leather collar up, ponytail tucked inside, and his only hat, a Dominion Paper baseball cap, pulled so low the brim touched the top of his glasses. The power of costumes. He felt like a spy.

There was a narrow alley between buildings, a shortcut to the next street over. Rhan jogged through the dark tunnel, the camera nudging him with every step.

Vic Ducharme got footage in Saudi Arabia, he told himself. You're in your own country on a Friday night.

Club Valhalla was not about money. It had probably been a series of unexceptional bars that had all failed, and now it was boxy, windowless, white sliding to gray, with a simple lighted sign. But as soon as he walked in, Rhan realized the owner didn't have to worry about customers.

The heat and music hit him in a solid blow, like walking into a blaring sauna. The crowd was stripped down—T-shirts, muscle shirts, even a girl in a metal bra. There was skin and leather and khaki and tattoos and so much metal Rhan imagined he could smell it, dull pewter that looked like iron, draped against skin in flared crosses and chains. And those boots—black, thick-soled and dangerous.

They were using them now, stomping in rhythm

with the raw gust of music that roared out from the band. The four musicians were sectioned off by a rope at the head of the room. Rhan could barely see them for the double row of people who chafed at the barrier, not dancing, not singing, but shouting back the words. *Do it, do it, do it…this time.*

He found himself standing on his toes, straining for a better view. Why was he so small here, he wondered, frustrated. Even the women seemed to tower over him. Was it the extra inch of the boots? Yet that didn't explain the power he sensed around him, a flow of energy that filled the room and lapped against the walls. He felt as if he were treading water.

It reminded him of Circle—if the whole gymnasium had been CTSR and all of them were wearing the same uniform.

Rhan began to move, threading his way through the half-naked bodies, feeling the moisture spreading out under his T-shirt, trickling down his back and ribs, gathering in the waistband of his jeans. He'd be swimming in the black leather soon, but he couldn't take it off.

He stopped when he saw Lee against the wall, back to it, arms folded over his chest. He was wearing a new jacket, brown leather, white button-down shirt and a tie, pulled loose but still knotted. Yet no one would have confused him with a junior exec or retail clerk—the Iceman didn't have that kind of face. Rhan wondered where he'd been tonight that he'd needed a disguise.

Lee was talking to a girl on his left, but his attention was on the whole room. Rhan could almost see the watchfulness spread out in a field around him, intensity warping the air the way heat made a highway shimmer. When his glance fell over Rhan, there was no surprise; he'd probably seen him walk in. The sweaty spy pushed his way irritably across the packed floor. Just once, he thought. Just once he'd like to catch that guy *first*.

And then he saw his shot. Across the room Jim Rusk was leaning casually, easily over a table, laughing and talking, campaigning with shaven, rough-edged men like the ones Rhan had seen all through Marlene's tapes. Skinheads. This was the piece of tape she wanted—and he couldn't get it. If he pulled the camera out in this crowd, he'd never make it to the door.

So think, Van! Look for something, a blind. He glanced around and saw two hallways off the main room. One seemed to lead to the kitchen, the other, he guessed, to the bathrooms. That hallway was bound to be busier but the angle was better; he'd have a direct line on Jim Rusk. And he only needed a few seconds.

It wasn't the washrooms. There was a door at the end that said Office, and there was a pinball game. Its flashing board was the only light in the darkened hall.

Rhan had never played pinball. He'd battled just

about everything else in an arcade, even the race-tracks, even the jerky, poor-quality, live-action shoot 'em ups. But pinball had never appealed to him. It was only...machinery. Too easy. There was nothing hidden, no secrets, all the mechanics out in front of you. It had never seemed challenging. Flip a ball around, light the lights. Big deal. That wasn't magic.

And yet as he stood there, he was swept up in a rush of nostalgia and memory. The game was God of Thunder—ideal for Club Valhalla—but he had his own memories of Thor with his bulging muscles, streaming yellow hair and magic hammer. Thor had never been one of his top heroes but his friend Darryl had inherited a big box of Marvel comics from the seventies, and the collection was loaded with Thor. He remembered those afternoons when they were kids, going through the box of faded colored newsprint, complaining about the artwork, laughing about the cover prices but devouring every story, every hero, one after the other like a banquet. And the argument that was never settled, never finished—who was the very best guy of all time and if you could have the powers of any of them, any one of them at all...

"You couldn't do it. No patterns."

Damn! He'd been caught again.

Rhan turned. The Iceman was standing in the mouth of the hallway, his jacket gone, sleeves rolled up and tie tossed casually over his shoulder.

Rhan felt the tug of panic and guilt. Idiot! How was he going to get his shot of Jim Rusk now? He had to get Lee out of here, or get into the other hallway.

"You can learn a pattern—I'll give you that." Lee was walking toward the game. "But this is different. This takes skill."

"It's just machinery."

"It's random response," Lee said, and he leaned on the console, looking in at the playing field of bumpers, targets and pulsing lights. "Speed and velocity and aim. And timing. All the variables interacting second by second, countless combinations, and all you have is that one move: Hit the ball."

Rhan had his fingers resting on the metal band that edged the glass case, looking in, intrigued against his will. He could do random response. What about the fire at the ACA? That was random. He responded.

"Pinball is real," Lee continued softly. "What happens, happens. You're not playing against somebody else's brain, their idea of what *should* happen. This is physics. It's real life. That's the challenge." He looked up. "Did you get anything?"

Rhan blinked, remembering. "Nothing yet."

"I can't keep him here long. He won't stay…"

"I'm doing the best I can! I don't turn this on like a tap, you know," Rhan snapped.

"Especially if you don't want to," Lee said. He

turned away. He dug into his pocket and pulled out two quarters that he fed into the machine. It wasn't an invitation or a dare. He was playing for himself.

The silver ball popped into the track. Lee pulled back the plunger with a decisive snap and the ball shot forward, around the curve and dropped into play.

Rhan was amazed by how the board lit up, how his own eyes fastened onto the heavy, beautiful ball that ricocheted off the targets, slow as it fell and then machine-gun rapid as it danced between the bumpers. He was captivated by the solid chunking of hits, the bells that racked up the points. His fingers were still on the console; he could feel it.

The Iceman was tapping the flippers, revving gently as he waited for the ball to bounce down to the gate. Patiently he let it roll onto the flipper, then shot it back up to hammer between the targets, a skilled strike, the points ringing up like a slot machine. He was good.

"I wouldn't ask if it didn't matter," Lee said, his eyes never leaving the game. "I hate to ask anybody for anything."

Rhan knew that, but he couldn't stop the little jab.

"Since when did you care about somebody else's life?" he said.

"Things change."

The game lit him from underneath, a glowing silhouette against the dark hall. With his pale hair and white shirt he looked like a ghost.

"That girl you were talking to," Rhan said. "Is she the one?"

"What do you think?"

The ball was in dangerous territory, dancing near the gate. Lee's body tensed and twisted as he tried to hammer it out, fighting the ricochet that kept winging it back at him. Finally the angle changed and the ball zipped between the flippers and through the gate, lost.

"I think she is," Rhan said.

"Okay."

"Or maybe not," he tried again.

The Iceman grinned at him, brief and wicked. "Okay." He yanked the plunger and the second ball sailed into play.

Rhan knew he should leave, find another blind angle and get the tape he'd come here to get. But still he stood, enthralled by the brightly lit console, the movement, the vibrations coming up through his fingertips. He found himself tensing and leaning as the ball edged near the gate, the little burst of triumph as it shot back up to safety. It was only temporary. You knew the thing was coming back down, and maybe in a hurry. Rhan wasn't playing but it felt like his game.

It went on and on, rising tension and little bursts of release, the battle straining through him, points racking up on the scoreboard that he never even looked at. When the ball finally shot through the gate, they both laughed with relief.

"I thought I was going to play that baby 'til king-dom come," Lee said, shaking his head. But the third ball had just snapped onto the track when the Iceman suddenly straightened.

"That's my phone." Rhan couldn't hear any-thing over the noise of the bar, but Lee pushed off the console and began backing down the hall. "It's in my jacket. Play me out."

"What?" Rhan said.

"Play me out," Lee said again, and then he was gone, around the corner and into the raucous room.

Rhan hesitated. He should leave and get the footage he'd come for. But it was only one ball.

You'll probably lose it in a hurry anyway, he told himself. Yet as he positioned himself in front of the console, tested the flippers, he knew. He could do random response. He could do physics. Or he'd try.

Pull—release. The last ball soared around the curve; his eyes never left it.

It was so different! To feel every hit go through your arms and into your body, the solidness of it, action and reaction over and over.

He stopped trying to follow every frantic move of the ball—that was madness—but relaxed his vision to encompass the whole board. That was bet-ter. Here it came, down to the gate, get it, get it...bang on! The ball sailed up into bumper territo-ry, points clanging, clunking...

Ground level. The knight was running, the sword so

heavy he had to carry it with two hands. A broad sword. This would scare them, if he could make it in time. But he was in two places at once, running over the rough ground, sweating, harsh breaths, yet from somewhere far above he saw the Vikings hack through the fragile, melting wall of the fortress. Oh, God—oh, no! The knight stumbled from the piercing cut, sorrow like a knife. He was too late.

The Vikings poured through the breach, screaming in triumph, a dark, ragged army against the pristine ice. They surged through room after room, scavenging, destroying, bent only on one prize.

The monk. In that instant the knight was in front of the downcast, hooded figure, both hands gripping his broad sword. A cry of lust and war went up behind him—discovery. There was only one last defender between them and the treasure beyond price.

Then the holy man looked up, raised his hooded face...

...and the silver ball shot through the gate and clunked down into the belly of the machine. Game over. But Rhan hung on to the sides of the console, leaning against it, reeling from images and emotions, alarm grappling with disbelief.

Somehow he had to tell Lee that the target was Jim Rusk.

SIXTEEN

LEE and Jim were both gone. Rhan knew from a hasty glance around the room. But the alarm was still ringing in him, the danger felt real and now. He had to tell somebody.

Find a phone, he thought. No matter where Lee was, he had the cellular. There was a pay phone in the little lobby but he barely glanced at it as he pushed out the door. Nobody had to tell him this place wasn't safe.

The night caught him in a cold embrace, seized him in all the places still damp with sweat; the air smelled like snow. But he didn't even zip up the jacket as he sprinted away from the club.

He didn't understand this! Why was he seeing that awful man as a monk? Valuable beyond understanding. And the knight who was protecting the hooded man couldn't be him. Yet he remembered the weight of the heavy sword, and his desperate two-handed grip on it. This isn't my fight, he told the Universe again. This isn't my problem.

As he jogged down the little alley, the camera he'd forgotten about was suddenly thudding against his ribs. He felt sick. He didn't have good tape, or even bad. His first assignment and he'd failed completely. Marlene had believed in him. How could he go back empty-handed? At that moment he would have shot film of Jim Rusk eating pizza. Anything to prove that he'd been here, that he'd tried.

He burst out of the alley and slowed to a stop. The Bonneville was parked across the street, exactly where he'd passed it earlier. He glanced left and right. Where were they? An idea flared into sudden hope. Maybe he could still get his footage.

But he had a debt—he'd made a promise. Rhan ripped the top flap off his cigarette package and found a pen in Lee's pocket.

Thor's target is Gandhi. Be careful. R.

He hesitated, trying to find the right words.

I'm sorry, he scribbled at the bottom, although he hoped Lee would never know for what.

He tucked the strip under the windshield wiper blade on the driver's side, then stepped back into the shadow of the alley. His hands were cold; he rubbed them together before he pulled out the camera. He clicked on the low-light feature and panned down the empty street, rehearsing focus. When he heard the voices, his heart began to run.

They were walking side by side, approaching the Bonneville from the left; they'd taken the long way around from the club. Rhan pulled in tightly on Jim Rusk, cropping Lee out of the shot. He wasn't part of the bargain.

The man didn't look like the devil. He was excited about something, a good mood that made him look almost boyish. Rhan heard the words as if from a farther distance. He was living in the magic frame.

"So if Moody is right about the numbers, we're

looking at a turn-out of three and a half, four thousand. Four thousand! That's great. We only had six in Scarborough and it looked a million…"

"But Moody's a liar." Lee, off camera.

"Well, he's got to deliver half, anyway." The excitement dipped; Jim grew older in an instant. "You want something to eat?"

"I'm not hungry."

"Come on. Vitamin B, vitamin D…"

The strange words caught in Rhan's ears. They reminded him of Gran.

But now they were at the car. Rhan forgot himself and turned the camera on Lee—he had to see. The Iceman snatched the slip off the windshield. He read it in a glance, then stuffed it in his pocket. Like the moment in the club, his face registered no surprise, not even the barest flicker.

He knew. The bastard already knew!

Jim Rusk stepped into the magic frame, close.

"What is it?"

"Advertising," Lee said. "Garbage."

For a moment the man just looked at him, weighing the lie.

"Okay." He put his arm around Lee's shoulders and gently kissed the side of his face. "Let's go home."

In the shadow of the alley, the spy lowered the camera, still recording, dimly aware that he was filming pavement. But it didn't matter. Somewhere in his numb mind the revelation clicked into place.

This was not a father fixation.

Lee was scanning the street. "You know, I forgot to tell Danny something," he said.

"So phone him."

"It'll just take a minute." He backed away and tossed the keys to Jim. "Meet me in ten. In front."

And then he was gone, darting down the street like a blond gazelle.

"Be careful," Jim Rusk said, too softly to do any good.

He's going back to look for me, Rhan thought. The first gust, the first punch of anger. This was worse than betrayal; he'd been played for a fool. He'd risked his neck to come here, to get information Lee already had. And for that.

Rhan tucked the camera securely into its holster and zipped up the jacket to hold it in, safe. He turned and started toward the other end of the alley, the burn rising from his stomach to his face, spreading over his body as he gathered speed.

You want to play me, Iceman? I can do pinball, I can do real life. You want physics? You'll get physics.

He caught him in mid-stride, stepped out of the shadows and seized the front of the brown leather jacket. Dominion Paper surged through his arms and shoulders. He pulled Lee into the alley and slammed him against the brick wall.

"You son of a bitch!"

He pulled forward and slammed him again.

"Don't hit me!" Lee's face was bare with surprise and panic. "Don't make me bleed."

The coward. Rhan swung him around and thrust him hard against the opposite wall, his knuckles digging into the Iceman's collarbone.

"You knew. All that bullshit and you knew! I risked my ass to go in there...!"

Lee wasn't fighting back. He wasn't even struggling. Rhan was enraged. He wanted it, he wanted the excuse.

"And for what? Did you think I was going to protect your *boyfriend*?!"

He yanked him off the wall. They both staggered, unbalanced, and Lee fell back. Rhan stayed on his feet, hovering over him, one hand still clenching the brown leather. God damn him. Why wouldn't he fight back? To hell with the excuse.

"Don't hit me—I'm positive."

"About what, asshole?!"

Lee had had enough. His arm shot out, broke the hold so hard and fast that Rhan stumbled. Lee rolled out of reach and onto his knees, gasping.

"What the hell do you think? One step away from the big A. It'll come to you."

It did. Rhan felt the blow in his legs, like Conlan kicking his feet out, the ground coming up too fast. He put his hand on the brick wall to steady himself.

"Shit," he whispered.

"Yeah, shit," Lee said, getting up stiffly. He leaned against the wall. Rhan stared. Everything else that had happened tonight seemed sudden-ly...small. He was small. And the things he hadn't even admitted he envied—the car and the cell phone and the respect—were microscopic.

"It wasn't hard," Lee said. "I was in all the cat-egories. But I thought the power would make the difference. That's how it works for me—I can tell things. I thought I would *know*." He let out a breath that was almost a laugh. "You and me—I thought our kind was immortal."

Our kind. It was too close and it was not com-fortable. Rhan took an unconscious step back.

"It's not AIDS," he blurted. His mind was rac-ing, trying to salvage something from the grade twelve Family Life class he'd pretty much slept through. "HIV positive isn't AIDS."

Lee smiled grimly. "Maybe not to you." It faded. "It's in the mail, RanVan. And the rest of you can sit back and split hairs and do fundraisers while I figure out how I'm going to get through the next five years. Or three. Or two."

He took a step toward him, his pale face chiseled into the darkness. "Who's going to look after me? Who could stand to watch this, live through this? Who's going to give to me when I can't give any-thing back?" His voice faltered. "I don't want to die alone."

"I'm sorry."

"I don't need sorry! Tell me how to save his life."

Rhan told him everything, laid the vision out for

him, what he had seen and when. He stumbled when he got to the part about the fortress because he suddenly understood it, how ice could melt without fire or sunlight, how it could melt from the inside. But he didn't tell him about the knight.

When he mentioned the hooded monk, Lee almost smiled. "That's him," he murmured, but he didn't say why. He understood, too, treasure beyond price. Marlene had been right. Jim Rusk was a financial pipeline, a key money connection for many of the small groups in the province and even beyond. Phantom cells could act without a leader but if they wanted money, they had to go to Jim Rusk. And that's when the man's morals became uncompromising. He would pay for research, demonstrations, call-in numbers, even espionage, but he would not fund anything or anyone who even smelled of violence.

"It drives the skinheads insane," Lee said, his eyes lighting up. "They'd go to the contributors direct, but they don't know who they are. Hell, even I don't know."

Between them they had who and what and why—the problem was when. "There's got to be more," Lee insisted, grabbing his shoulder. "Think! What did you miss?"

Rhan pulled away, a knee-jerk of alarm that was so obvious he was embarrassed. As if the gangster could jump down his throat, or slip into his pocket. But knowing better didn't mean you could stop it.

"Stay away from crowds," Rhan said. It was a blind guess.

"That's a big help," Lee snapped. "Tomorrow's rally is between three and five thousand."

"So phone the psychic hotline," Rhan shot back. "Jesus! What do you expect from me? Did it ever occur to you that it's your own damn fault you're in this mess?!"

The Iceman looked at him in weary disbelief. "Only every day," he said. He started to walk away but a few steps down the alley, he turned.

"I need my jacket," he said.

Rhan felt a clutch of panic. He was still wearing the camera—he was supposed to be a spy.

"Now?"

"Yeah, now. Or he's going to think I sold it."

Rhan unzipped the jacket and twisted away, trying to shrug it off without Lee seeing his left side. "Sold it?" he repeated.

"I had a pretty famous drug problem," Lee said irritably, taking a step. "Save me a little grief for once. Just give it back."

Rhan gave another violent shrug and the jacket came off, and the camera dropped to the ground with a dull thud. He bent down quickly and scooped it up—not fast enough.

"What is that?" Lee blurted, but he knew. "What the fuck is that?!"

Rhan was backing away. "I didn't use it."

"Then give me the tape."

For the first time Rhan realized he had what Marlene wanted—a piece of tape to hang Jim Rusk with. He hadn't planned on showing it to anybody, but it was suddenly too valuable to give up.

It was valuable to the Iceman. He was advancing with his hand out, his face a mix of fury and alarm. He knew the possibilities.

"Give it to me!"

Fight or flight, and he couldn't come to blows with this man, not anymore.

Down the alley, down the deserted street, heart galloping, lungs burning, clutching the camera like Life itself, the icy November air freezing the sweat on his body, not even listening for footsteps because he was praying so hard. Make it to the car, make it to the car, oh, please, let me make it to the car...

"Vampire!"

The call seemed far behind him but Rhan didn't stop until he touched the back of the Mazda, until he leaned gasping on the trunk. He must have been traveling at the speed of light; Lee had given up almost a block behind him. Scared was way faster than mad.

"You vampire!" Lee called again, like a cry of pain. There was so much hate that even at a distance Rhan felt the kick of it, and he pushed angrily off the car. He didn't know what he was going to throw back but he had lots of choices. Junkie. Nazi. Queer.

"I thought you were better than me!" Lee screamed.

Rhan stopped in the road. He suddenly couldn't speak, couldn't open his mouth. His skin was on fire.

He got in the car, his trembling hand thrust the key in the ignition. But as he pulled away, the rearview mirror caught one glimpse of the heart-broken man still standing in the road, face in his hands.

SEVENTEEN

HE walked straight to the shower as soon as he reached his suite, pausing only to set down the camera and turn on one light. Under the water he kept inching the temperature up, hot to the edge of pain. He scrubbed at his body, the sweat that had dried on him like a second skin, and washed his hair twice, three times. Then he just stood under the steady stream as the warmth dimmed and faded away. But it was no good; he couldn't make himself feel clean. Lee Dahl might be a lot of things, but he wasn't a liar.

So why do you care what he thinks? Rhan told himself. You've been mad as hell at the stupid ass for...days. He screwed up his life and God knows who else's. He knows this is his own fault.

But fault was such a useless, empty word. It didn't stop Rhan's stomach from plummeting, even now. There were worse people in the world than Lee Dahl, and they'd live on and on. He couldn't believe he lived in a universe that felt Lee Dahl needed to be punished. The Iceman didn't deserve his gangster any more than Gran had deserved hers. And he didn't deserve to be used, his personal life flashed on TV so a student cameraman could get a name credit.

It had seemed so simple earlier today. Sitting in Marlene's office, her excitement painting his future in bright colors right there in front of him. Oh, God, he'd wanted it. And all the questions explained away with one blessing. Just tell the truth. It had sounded like the easiest, most noble thing in the world.

Except the truth only worked if you told all of it, Rhan thought. The camera should have been filming in the alley, trained on that frightened man who didn't want to die alone. It should have been on the hitman who'd lured Jim and Lee out in the first place, his weapon hidden under his jacket. That man wasn't a knight or even someone Rhan liked.

I'll destroy the tape, Rhan told the Universe. I'll film over it, or erase it. I'll tell Marlene they never showed up.

But even as he thought it, he felt the tug of doubt. It was valuable. It would get him money or notoriety or even a job. How could he destroy something that valuable?

He was sitting on his pulled-out bed wearing only sweatpants, on top of the tumbled blankets and sheets, smoking a cigarette. He was alone but he didn't feel it. It seemed as if something was here with him, that one little piece of information he'd kept to himself, suddenly so huge that it took up the whole room.

But the knight isn't me, he told the Universe. It couldn't be. I don't even agree with these people, and I'm only one guy.

He remembered the Viking dance floor, thundering boots and the gush of raw energy that threatened to drown him, so much and so powerful it lapped against the walls.

A sound made him jump. It took him a second to realize someone was knocking at the door to his suite. He was surprised and suddenly wary. It was almost midnight and he'd been in dangerous country tonight. He pulled a T-shirt from one of his piles, not caring whether it was clean or dirty.

Hand on the doorknob, he paused. "Who is it?"

"CTSR Lost and Found," Jen said.

He swung the door open, astonished. Jen had his jacket over one arm. He'd never gone back to the studio to retrieve it. But she was carrying her own coat, too, hugging them both nervously. How long had she been here?

"I came earlier but you weren't home," she explained, then gestured at the upper suite. "Your neighbors found me. Charmaine made me stay for coffee, twisted my arm. We heard you come in but I waited until the shower stopped running." She grinned. "I think you set a record."

He was still so surprised that he said nothing. Jen shifted uneasily.

"Well, here it is," she said, handing over his jacket. "Maybe you should have a string on it, like mittens."

"Thanks," Rhan said blankly. God, she was so pretty.

She looked embarrassed. "I guess you're telling me to go home?"

"No!" He landed on the planet again. "I mean, do you want to come in?"

He felt the usual pang when she walked into the kitchen. "It's as bad as last time," Rhan said, trying to clear a place for her to put her coat.

"Actually, it's worse," Jen said. "Would...would you just sit down for a minute?"

There was a catch in her voice. Rhan sat on the edge of the bed, wondering. Jen leaned against the wall, looking in his direction but not quite at him.

"I wanted you to know that you were right today," she said. "I mean, why should you trust me? You don't know me. And not everybody deserves the truth."

The words caught on him—he believed in that.

"But I guess I'm sort of paranoid. I mean, I really, really like you and...lies make me nervous. I'd rather know the worst right away. I was married once." She shrugged and tried to smile, but it froze on her face. "I got out alive."

His line, but it wasn't a joke. Rhan felt the news in his stomach. She was only his age, or maybe a year older. He didn't have to ask what kind of marriage came and went like a cyclone, because he knew. He felt nailed to the edge of the bed.

"Did you have kids?" he blurted.

"Oh, no, thank God. That would have been a disaster." She shook her head thinking about it. "A *worse* disaster."

"Does he bother you?" Rhan said. His voice

seemed to be spiraling down, as if he was running out of air. "Follow you?"

"Not…lately."

"Restraining order?" he whispered.

She looked into his eyes for the first time. "You know this. How do you know this?"

"I'm one of those worse disasters," Rhan said.

For a moment Jen held his gaze. Then she suddenly looked up. She was smiling, almost laughing.

"Okay! I get it," she told the ceiling. "I figured it out." Back to him. "You were so familiar I was sure I had met you somewhere. Even that first night, at Devon's. That's why I grabbed your shoulder. I thought I knew you."

"Not because I was cute?"

Then she did laugh. She dropped onto the bed to sit beside him. "It was driving me crazy. I went through my old yearbooks, right down to junior high, looking for you."

"No, we went to that *other* school together," Rhan said.

The room sobered. "Yeah, we did," Jen said.

He found her hand the same moment she was reaching for his. "Tell me," she said.

And he did, from the beginning, as much as he knew. He was amazed, not because it was easy but because it was safe. The reactions that he feared the most—horror and pity and distance—weren't there. Jen's marriage might have been different from his parents', but she'd been in that country,

Rhan thought. She knew the landscape.

And she understood things that he didn't.

"Because it doesn't happen in a day," Jen said. "It's little by little. 'Where are you going?' 'Who's going to be there?' 'Don't be so...goddamn stupid.'" She bit her lip. "You start avoiding those things so he won't get mad. Except there's always something new. So you have to avoid those, too. And then more things. And then one morning you wake up and realize you're living in this straight line, like a dark hallway, and all the doors are closed. You don't even know how you got there. But how couldn't you know?! And you think, I really must be...stupid."

"No, you're not," Rhan said, the heat rushing to his face. "You're smart and you're brave and you did the best you could." He didn't understand the feeling that swept through him, a relief like putting something down he didn't even know he'd been holding. His heart was in his throat but he couldn't stop running the words through his mind. You did the best you could. They were potent, powerful, enormous.

"Well, I didn't do it alone," Jen said hesitantly. He looked at her again. "That's sort of what I came here to say. Incredible things seem to happen around you, and if you don't want to tell anybody, that's okay. But I notice them because...a miracle happened to me, once."

Miracle. It was a big word, and not one that he used often.

"It was the last day," Jen said quietly. "It was pretty bad. He'd been drinking all day and just…getting meaner. I kept thinking, Should I go? Should I go? But I was afraid he would chase me and then it would be worse." She almost smiled to herself. "You think, it's not so bad if you can still stand it.

"Then, around one in the morning, everything changed. He stopped yelling and swearing and just started throwing my clothes over the balcony. I thought, Oh, my God, it's going to be me. I ran into the bedroom and locked the door. It just had one of those little locks in the handle. I was so scared it wouldn't hold. I picked up the phone and I dialed 911 and got an operator. And right while I'm talking to her, boom! he kicks at the door. I was so shocked I jumped back three feet. And then I see for the first time that he'd already cut the phone cord. It was dangling there, against my leg. There was no way I could be talking to that operator but I *was*. And they got somebody out to the apartment in four minutes."

She bit her lip and shrugged. "So nobody believed me. My mom and my sisters, they thought I'd ripped the cord out when I jumped, but it doesn't matter. Because I know what I know." Her eyes were bright, liquid. "That was the day I realized all the doors were open."

Rhan was sitting very still. He was touched with awe, by her story, by her quiet acceptance. I know what I know. She didn't have to tell him it was one of those life corners because he could see it. To go from that woman hiding in the bedroom to the one interrogating the director of fine arts against a fire truck was a huge leap, bigger than any he'd ever made. That qualified as a miracle, too.

He brought her hand suddenly to his lips. He'd never done that in his life, never imagined it, but in that moment it was exactly what he wanted to say.

Jen was taken aback. "Oh, sure. Be wonderful. Fight dirty." She threw her free arm around his neck and kissed the side of his face. He twisted around to meet her, kiss her back, emotion and desire igniting in a flare. She put her hand on his thigh. He couldn't stop the rush of his breath, his voice.

"That's what I love about you," she said huskily. "Enthusiasm."

He loved everything about her, the heat of her skin, the smell of her hair, the curvy softness that was utterly female. He loved the brave young woman wrapped up inside it. His enthusiasm was lifting him right off the planet. But he knew all too well that he wasn't immortal; neither of them were. He managed to pull himself back, still wearing some of his clothes.

"You know…I wasn't…I don't have…"

Jen smiled; with her tousled hair she looked like a naughty sprite. She reached into her purse on the floor and put the little packet into his hand.

"I never needed a string on my mittens," she said.

It was not like any other time. To touch someone you cared about, Rhan thought, to feel safe enough to talk out loud, to look into a face that looked back into you, to want and be wanted—was the most exciting embrace he knew.

He was already swimming in desire and sensation, but a single pulse kept flashing through him, like a ray of light that cut through a churning sea to the murky bottom. He was not alone. She knew his secrets and he knew hers. This was what it was like not to be alone.

And that changed everything.

"Please stay," he said later. They were lying quietly in the dark, tangled up in the sheets and each other; he couldn't stop touching her. "Please."

Jen was silent, thinking. "Not…yet. But sometime, maybe. When I'm really sure." She yawned, but it dissolved into a sleepy chuckle. "See? You're not that exciting."

He yawned, too. "Neither are you."

There were minutes of warm silence that he just lay in like a bath.

"Don't fall asleep," Jen said dreamily. "You have to drive me home."

"Right away," Rhan promised, a murmur against her bare shoulder.

◆

Moe Gervais had taught him to drive. Moe was the

best mechanic Rhan knew; he was the best at a lot of things. He'd taught Rhan to drive an automatic transmission at sixteen but it was only last winter that he'd shown up at the Trail's End with the silver Mazda.

"Come on," Moe said. He was wearing a gray parka over his grease-stained coveralls, and a short, red toque half-perched on his head. He was not someone who worried about how he looked.

"It's snowing," Rhan said, but he was looking at the icy road, gouged with ruts and dusted with powder.

"If you can drive a standard in this, you can drive anything, anywhere," Moe said. Rhan felt a tug of apprehension, but he couldn't disappoint this man. He got his coat.

Swinging into the passenger seat, he asked Moe whose car it was.

"Mine, now, thanks to the Garage Keeper's Act," the mechanic said. That meant someone had brought the car in for work and never paid for it. Moe had filed a claim that let him keep the car for the debt.

Zipping in and out of traffic, watching Moe expertly thrust through the gears, Rhan wondered how anyone could have left this great little car behind.

They drove to a distant mall. Retail business was really bad in February; the parking lot was almost empty. With the engine running, they switched seats. Rhan slid in behind the wheel and his mood lifted immediately. He liked this car, the low, gutsy rumble of the engine's idle, the extra dials on the dash. It felt fast.

Moe had him push in the clutch and trace through the H-shaped channel of gears. Shifting didn't seem that hard.

"You're watching the tach but you're listening to the engine," Moe said, pointing an oil-stained finger at the dial that was the tachometer. "It red-lines at two thousand revs, but you'll hear it, you'll come to feel it." He grinned. "A standard you drive with the seat of your pants."

"Okay," Rhan said.

"And never forget the clutch," Moe cautioned. "You try to shift without the clutch in and you'll strip the gears. That's big time."

"Okay," Rhan said, a little impatiently. He was eager to start.

"Clutch in, shift to first, take your foot off the brake."

Rhan did, and promptly stalled it.

"All right, again," Moe said. And Rhan did it again, exactly. The third time he managed to lurch forward a few feet before the car cut to silence. Rhan fired the engine up once more, swearing under his breath, sweat gathering under his clothes. God, this was embarrassing.

"Just relax," Moe said calmly. "You'll get it."

And he did, eventually. He navigated slowly

around and around the mall, trying to learn the dance of clutch and shift and gas and brake while he struggled with the icy road. There were stop signs and intersections in the parking lot. Moe made him go through them all. Each time he had to start from the beginning, the touchy moment between neutral and first gear. Even as he got better there were relapses; he had to concentrate all the time.

"A standard you *drive*," Moe said, but kindly. "Everything else is just steering."

Rhan was thrilled when he finally managed an untroubled circuit of the mall, once, then twice. Yet when Moe told him to pull over, he didn't argue. His shoulders were knotted from the tension; he was glad to be finished for the day. Moe got out and Rhan opened the driver's door, ready to change seats. To his astonishment, Moe kept walking.

"It's yours for five hundred," the mechanic called over his shoulder.

"Dollars?" Rhan squeaked with disbelief. It was a fraction of what the car was worth.

"You just have to drive it home," Moe called. For the first time Rhan noticed the dark-green truck parked discreetly at the edge of the lot. Moe's truck. He'd meant to do this all along, planned to leave him here! In that moment Rhan almost hated him.

He clutched the frame of the open door, peering over the car's roof at the gray parka and red toque that were growing smaller by the second. It was one thing to tool around a parking lot; it was another to drive through real traffic on slippery roads, with dozens of stop lights and a thousand chances for humiliation, or worse. Yet to have a car, Rhan thought, a car of his *own*.

"I don't know if I can do this," he blurted, but Moe was too far to hear him now. He waved as he climbed into the truck. And Rhan realized the time for wondering was gone. He was a long way from home and he had to get back. Somehow, he had to get back.

EIGHTEEN

HE woke up happy, luxurious contentment smooth over his body, the comfortable peace of having slept long and well. He had three seconds of it before he sat bolt upright.

"Oh, shit!" He was supposed to drive Jen home. Now it was morning and she was gone. He threw the covers off and called her name, on the off-chance she was hiding in his one closet.

You jerk, Van, he told himself, heart sinking as he groped around for his glasses. You idiot jerk.

But a note was on the table.

I fell asleep, too! I have to babysit for my sisters today so I took the C-train. Call me later. Jen. There was a phone number and one more line scribbled at the bottom. *You know I only love people I love.*

And that was him. He read the note over and over, the wonder spreading through his chest. Me, too, he thought, and he suddenly wanted to tell her, had to tell her. He glanced at the clock and dialed the number. Ten o'clock was "later," wasn't it? Busy signal. He paced the room and smoked a cigarette that really wasn't necessary; his blood was already singing in his veins. He'd waited nineteen years but he could hardly wait another minute.

The line was still busy. He took a shower but he had trouble shaving. He kept grinning at his reflection. He looked like a goof with a secret. He even cut himself once, and he hadn't done that in years. Some mornings you didn't wake up with the same face.

Still busy. A house full of women, he thought, but he was calmer now, the news permeating in a slow warmth through his body. This wasn't going away. He'd get his chance. He didn't have anything else to do today.

Well, one thing. Rhan walked over and picked up the camera. All the wondering was gone, blown away in the night. He was going to bulk-erase the tape. He knew he could film over it but he was suddenly anxious to obliterate it, wipe it out as if it had never happened. He dressed quickly, tied back his hair and pulled on his jacket. He still wanted that exciting career Marlene had talked about, but he wouldn't ruin lives to get it.

The day was cold, gray and overcast. It didn't matter. Rhan tipped the clerk at the convenience store the entire price of the coffee.

"Wow, did you win the lottery?" the clerk teased.

"Better than that," Rhan said.

Rounding the corner with his steaming cardboard cup in one hand, the camera in the other, he stopped. The Superman poster was still hanging at The Odyssey but they'd changed the rest of the display. In the window he saw a single chainmail gauntlet for the right hand—metal sleeve and leather glove with the fingers cut out. Heavy and beautiful, it looked old—it looked real. He loved it instantly, but the price tag made him catch his breath. That was real, too.

Don't be stupid, you can't afford it, he told himself. It's kid stuff anyway and…what would you do with it? But the adult truth didn't change the bare rush of desire. He loved it—he wanted it.

"Oh, shirtless hell. Just buy it."

Rhan whirled around, his heart thumping. Some voices you didn't forget, didn't mistake, not the ones that you'd heard your whole life. He was alone on the street.

"Where are you?" he whispered, hope still flickering inside him. There was no answer, not the slightest rustle of air. But he knew what he'd heard.

"A perfect fit—it must be yours," the shop owner said, laughing. With his jacket on, only the leather across his hand could be seen. It looked like an odd biking glove. But the weight of it was on his arm, indelible, the clingy metal links pressing against him, reminding him at the slightest movement. He felt a burst of old, familiar joy. He felt six years old and ten feet tall. He had one arm in the Magic Nation.

Luckily he was also nineteen with a charge card. "I guess it is mine," he said.

Out on the sidewalk again, he paused.

"Thanks," he said out loud to the Universe.

Classes weren't in session on Saturdays but H Building was open and busy—students and instructors taking advantage of the equipment to do catch-up. In the editing room, Rhan found two Second Years hovering in front of the bulk-eraser.

"Riley screwed it up," the first one snapped.

"And I'm fixing it! Don't get your intestines in a knot."

Rhan was untroubled. He believed in everyone today, and this gave him another chance to try Jen. He left his coffee and the camera on the table and found the pay phones in the hallway. The hand that punched in the numbers had leather across the knuckles, a thin line of metal at the wrist. It made him bold.

Success! His heart was pumping after the second ring. But when the phone was picked up, he heard a cacophony of children, yelling, crying, and a squeaky little voice demanded, "Who is this?"

He wondered what to say—after all, they didn't know him—when he heard a frazzled Jen in the background.

"Put him down...put him down *right now*!"

Rhan felt a dip of disappointment; not a perfect ambiance.

"Tell your auntie Jen I'll phone her later," he said carefully.

"But who is it?" the girl insisted, four years old and relentless.

The guy who loves her, Rhan thought. The guy who wants to be a great cameraman *and* a great human being, because of her.

"Her best friend," he said, and hung up.

He went back to the editing room. Only Riley was left, still fussing with the bulk-eraser. Riley and Rhan's cup of coffee.

Rhan felt the blow in his stomach.

"Where's my camera?"

"What?" the Second Year said, twisting around.

"A little camcorder! It was right here!"

"Well, shit, I don't know. I've been working..."

Rhan took a step. "That other guy, where'd he go?"

"Martin? He's in check-out."

Rhan was running, down the hall, down the stairwell to the basement. He was trying not to panic but he felt sick. He didn't know what worried him more, the thought of losing the camera or the tape falling into the wrong hands—any hands.

Martin's back was to him in the narrow hallway that was the equipment check-out. Rhan seized his shoulder and whipped him around, harder than he meant.

"The camera?!"

Martin was startled, eyes wide, almost frightened. "She took it," he said hurriedly. "She said it was hers!"

"Who?"

"Marlene Foye..."

Rhan let him go. He was running again, mouth dry, body empty and weightless. He wasn't thinking, only counting, how many stairwells and hallways from the basement to the second floor.

Marlene had her coat on, locking the door to the Communications office. He could see the tape in her hand. Her face lit up like Las Vegas when she saw him charge into the hall.

"You are getting *paid* for this," she bubbled. "It's better than I dreamed! I mean, he kisses his lieutenant? This will shake up their whole community, from Vancouver to..."

"You can't use it," Rhan cut her off, gasping. "You just can't."

"What are you talking about?"

"I was going to erase it. You can't use it," he said again.

"This is my tape, shot on my camera during an assignment you accepted from me," Marlene said, suddenly an icy professional. "You bet your ass I'll use it."

Rhan took a step and her whole demeanor changed. Her body straightened as she tucked the tape safely into her shoulder bag. But he didn't care if he looked threatening.

"You'll...ruin them," Rhan said.

Her eyes flashed. "And just what were you going out to get? A promo spot? I'm sorry about your friend, but you're the one who set this up, remember?"

A jab of pain twisted his stomach. He was.

"You can't pick and choose, Rhan. If you go out looking for the truth, you have to be prepared to find it." She was backing away now, toward the other end of the hallway, the other exit. "If you don't have the balls for it, better stay in the studio, where it's nice and safe."

She whirled around, not running but a purposeful stride. Rhan's mind leapt to the one tiny space it had not dared go before.

"And what if they die?" he called out. "What if somebody pulls them out of the Bow River?"

The *Wunderkind* paused at the exit, her hand on the door, and looked back at him, her beautiful face unbelievably clear.

"Wouldn't you call that justice?" she said. Then she pushed out through the door.

"No," Rhan said out loud in the hallway. But it was too late. The damage would be done and all he could do was warn them. He flew down to the main level, to the row of phones. Trembling, he punched in the string of numbers he hadn't even realized he'd memorized.

It rang and rang. He clung to the receiver, refusing to give up. Finally the recording came on. "This cellular customer is away from the phone. If you'd like to leave a message..."

The beep. "Lee—" Rhan hesitated, then he felt pressure behind him, like wind at his back, unseen energy pushing him forward. The words tumbled out, as if on their own. "For God's sake, keep him out of the crowd. I'm on my way. You're going to have to trust me."

He hung up, dazed, his heart still running. As

soon as he'd said it, he'd known it was true. This was the day and that was the crowd. Somehow when the army broke through the fortress he had to be standing in front of Jim Rusk. It didn't make sense—he was only one guy—but he had to be there, with a sword so heavy he could only hold it with two hands.

He burst into Mark's office. The instructor looked up, startled.

"I need a BetaCam. Today. Right now."

"Why?"

Rhan took a breath. "You're going to have to trust me."

The sky seemed like a solid thing, a blanket of gray dough, as Rhan maneuvered the Mazda through traffic toward Prince's Island Park. The gauntlet was still on his arm, but he just felt small and mortal now. He didn't know if Lee had gotten the message, or if he believed it. The Iceman would probably as soon choke him as look at him.

Still blocks from the park, the streets were clogged with people moving forward on foot. There were regular people—students, mothers carrying placards instead of children, Christian Youth—as well as the shaved, white and khaki uniforms he'd seen before, all made taller by the big boots, made bold by swastikas and flared-edge crosses. And there was something he'd only heard about—young men with black X's painted on their cheeks, across their hands, or taped to their shoulders in electrician's tape. Straight edge guys. They reminded him of the Viking skinheads, except for the insignia.

Rhan parked the car and pulled the big black case out of the back seat. He took a deep breath and joined the throng.

Police cars clustered on the street where the bridge led to the island park. There was a bottleneck of people at the entrance—many were being pulled aside and checked for weapons—but it was inside the park that he felt the first pulse of alarm. There were way more than five thousand people.

A stage was set up at one end of the open area; beside it was a portable unit, a little trailer half the size of a mobile home. Rhan guessed that's where the speakers were waiting. A band had been on the stage but they were packing up, everything but the amplifiers. All along the edge of the field were the voyeurs: city police, park security, both television stations, an ambulance and medical personnel. And in the field the crowd was divided into camps, but flowing like a single, snarling, liquid creature.

A sudden shout of curses made him turn. A black X seized a Viking by the ears and brought the shaved head down on his knee, hard and fast. Police leapt from the sidelines, a small army to pull the men apart and keep any more squalls from flaring up. Blood poured over the white shirt from the Viking's nose.

The sight of it sent a shockwave through Rhan's body. Like on the dance floor of Club Valhalla he seemed to be drowning, surrounded by a raw swirl of violent energy. Clustered in groups, caught in one small field, the opposing forces amplified each other. Even the placard mothers were swearing, swaggering, filled with power. How could he ever hold this back? Rhan wondered. It was so big and he was only one guy.

"You're not alone, you're just in front."

The voice wasn't Gran's but it was as real, as familiar and comforting. In that instant he could feel the energy behind him again, protecting his back and pushing him forward at the same time. Okay, Rhan told the Universe. I'll do what I'm here to do. He struggled through the crowd to be in the first line, dead center in front of the stage.

He dropped to one knee and opened his case. Inserting the tape, his hands felt numb, frozen, even the one with leather across the knuckles. God, it was cold. For the first time he noticed flecks of white against the dark surface of the case. It was snowing—not big friendly flakes but hard little crystals that skittered when they hit. Ice.

When he stood up he saw Lee Dahl. He was standing next to the platform between the speakers' trailer and the stage. Under the leaden sky, above the black leather and white shirt, his face looked gaunt, colorless. But he was watching the crowd with an intensity Rhan could sense twenty paces away, a devotion that was humbling in this field smoldering with hate. This was not just a job.

Rhan hoisted the camera onto his shoulder, knowing it would obscure his face. He wasn't sure if the Iceman had seen him yet, or what he'd do if he did.

The crowd started to roar as soon as the door to the portable unit opened. Rhan caught Jim Rusk in his lens and followed him, past Lee, up the stairs, onto the stage. In a gray suit, he looked like any politician, maybe younger, maybe more handsome, but not a monster and not a monk, not a treasure beyond price.

Jim Rusk set his papers on the podium, then leaned forward in a sudden plea. "I want to welcome every one of you, because you all care about your country. For that country, and for your own safety, please, I beg you—let's have a peaceful afternoon."

The cheering dipped into a discontented rumble. It wasn't what anybody wanted to hear. But they were the last words Rhan remembered because he was concentrating hard on the figure in his lens, even as he felt his attention focus on something else. It was like a nudge of pressure far behind him, sharp but distant, and it was getting closer. Rhan's heart leapt. He knew this was the One. The urge to turn around and look was very strong.

Stay on shot, he ordered himself. That's the only protection you can give him. Don't leave him, for anything.

The crowd was chanting now, the vibrations

buffeting his body like gusts of wind. Ice crystals were stinging every inch of exposed skin and he couldn't feel his fingers, yet still he hung on with both hands. The One was closer now, much closer, halted but pacing with nervous energy, lust and anger and frustration.

The field erupted, cheers or rage or both. Jim Rusk was finished; the next speaker was striding onto the stage. Rhan followed Rusk with the camera down the platform steps, past the spot where Lee had been standing, but wasn't anymore. Where the hell had he gone?

Beside the platform, someone handed Rusk a military poncho with a hood that he pulled on over his suit against the biting snow. The crowd was calling to him now, calling him into it.

Rhan felt the sudden acceleration behind him, burning pressure like a hot poker between his shoulders. Oh, God, he's here, Rhan thought. He's right here. Rusk pulled up his hood and started toward the people who wanted him so desperately.

The knight and the Viking moved in the same instant. RanVan felt him at his back, his shoulders taking the brunt of fury and frustration. Death was in this man's hand and he had the heart to do it. It took everything the knight had not to turn around.

The monk looked up, startled by the movement, by the men and the camera that was suddenly in his face.

"Mr. Rusk, I need to talk to you!" RanVan blurted.

The square-jawed face inside the hood was defensive. "I'm not giving interviews today," he said, preparing to step aside.

"Please, Mr. Rusk!" The pressure was unbearable, like the point of a huge wedge and he was holding it all back. How could he make this man understand?! "I'm…like Lee."

The face changed, softened. "Rhan Van," Rusk said. "He thinks the world of you."

"Coward!" the Iceman cried.

The voice came from the right, from the other side of the stage, a taunt full of loathing. It was meant to hurt and it did. Jim Rusk turned to look. Lots of people turned.

"You want somebody? Come and get me."

Behind the viewfinder, the knight's face was burning. He was supposed to take this? The urge to turn around and lash out, fight back, was almost irresistible.

Stay on shot, stay on shot! He forced the words through his mind like a chant. He was stretched to breaking but he wouldn't let go of his sword.

"Come on, you gutless bastard!"

Abruptly the pressure behind Rhan was gone.

"Go now!" Rhan whispered. "Into the trailer. Now!"

The monk turned and fled, gray-green rain cape flapping. Rhan waited until Rusk was safely inside before he hoisted the camera off his shoulder. It felt like the weight of the world after all this time. He was trembling, from the strain, from the danger that had been pressed up against him. He dropped tiredly to one knee as he set the camera down.

But you did it! The triumph shot up inside his weary body. You hung on and you saved his life, even if nobody appreciates it.

Then a woman screamed. The sound stopped the speaker on the platform in mid-sentence. It yanked Rhan to his feet and pulled him over the cold grass, faster and faster, shoving people out of his way, around the side of the stage to the right.

Lee was against the wooden wall. He looked so surprised. People nearby had gathered into a stunned circle, staring in disbelief at the pale man in the black leather jacket who clutched at his chest between his ribs, a brilliant red river gushing down his white shirt.

Rhan stumbled from the sudden pain. Oh, God—oh, no!

The crowd was close and creeping closer with a sick fascination. Rhan felt a gust of fury.

"AIDS!" he shouted. "He has AIDS."

This time the truth worked. People pulled back in panic, the gangster more terrifying than the horror in front of them. Rhan broke through the circle.

"Is he safe?" Lee gasped.

In that instant Rhan realized he *hadn't* been alone, only in front. The Iceman hadn't been yelling at him, he'd been calling the killer, diverting the thrust of hate onto himself. Rhan felt humbled for a second time. He knew the word for this kind of devotion.

"Yes," he said.

Lee nodded a thank you, but even that effort drained him. He slid down the wall to a sitting position. Rhan dropped helplessly to his knees. He didn't know what to do.

"Don't touch the blood," Lee warned.

Over the sound system they were calling for the medics. But they were across the field, a world away. Rhan desperately wanted to do something. Red had washed down most of the man's body but his left foot was clear of it. Rhan put his hand on that foot and held on.

Lee's face looked translucent, but the fear seemed to leap out of his eyes. "I don't want to die alone," he blurted.

"No," Rhan promised.

"Don't let me go alone."

"No," Rhan whispered. He was squeezing that foot so hard, trying to will color and life back into this body, praying for one last piece of magic.

The police came and pushed the crowd back farther and Rhan wouldn't let go. The field was buzzing as the news ran through it, and above the rushing sound Rhan heard a cry, not alarm or fear but the knife-edge of loss from the only human being on the planet who could mean it. Still he wouldn't let go. And when the paramedics came, fully equipped for the containment of the catastrophe, news of the disease grim in their faces, they looked at Rhan with disbelief. And finally they made him let go.

NINETEEN

THE thing about pinball, Rhan realized, was that you could not win. You could win for awhile, earn replays and keep on lighting the lights, racking up points that sounded as solid as real coins clunking down out of a slot machine, a cascade of Good Money. But there was no ultimate prize, no screen that came up and said, "Congratulations! The treasure is won, the universe saved and the Evil One destroyed."

You could play pinball for what felt like an eternity, play it brilliantly and beautifully, a magic man of skill and aim, and still there would come the moment when the silver ball shot through your best efforts, through the gate and into the belly of the machine.

"I don't understand," Rhan told Jen. "I did everything I was supposed to. I did it *right*. But for what? I just don't understand."

She didn't have any answers but she listened to him, over and over, as many times as he had to say it. It helped but he was still haunted. He'd had the vision, the cryptic preview. He'd had one arm in the Magic Nation and blue lightning at his back, all the powers of the Universe protecting him, holding him up.

And the best I could do was sit beside him so he didn't have to die alone, Rhan thought. He didn't feel like a knight or a Master Number; he didn't feel like a great cameraman or a great anything.

The Foye Report, "A Nation of Hate," aired Monday. Rhan knew his footage was on it, but he didn't watch. He was sure the documentary was good; the *Wunderkind* knew a lot about inhumanity.

Tuesday at noon he trooped out of Studio A with the rest of the class and saw Jim Rusk waiting for him at the end of the hallway. No politician's suit this time—jeans and a jacket and a briefcase. Younger clothes, older face. It seemed to Rhan that no amount of money would erase those lines.

Mark was locking the studio but he hung back, stalling. He recognized the man with the briefcase.

Jim came up to Rhan and for a few minutes they talked about things they both understood. The Viking murderer had been apprehended at the edge of the park. Prosecution wouldn't be a problem; there were at least four witnesses.

"I guess I'm glad but...it doesn't really help, does it?" Rusk said wearily.

"No," Rhan agreed.

"You know, I'm fighting with his family for the body. They didn't want him when he was alive." A bitter smile flickered and was gone. "I just wish I understood. I mean, why now? Why this? It's not fair! If you knew what demons that kid had already beaten..." The man's voice twisted and almost broke.

Rhan knew the Iceman's demons, some in person and some only by name. He didn't have that answer they both needed so badly.

Yet he heard himself say, "No one is wasted. We're all too...important."

Jim Rusk looked at him. "Do you have access to a camera? There's something I'd like you to do for me."

The cardboard cityscape was already lit for single subject.

"Do you want to be camera or control?" Mark said. It made Rhan smile. Mark was probably the only man in the building who could handle the entire control booth—buttons and levers and reels—all by himself.

"I'll do camera," he said. As he lined up his shot of Jim Rusk sitting calmly with his briefcase, he had a sense of history in the room. He had no idea what the man was going to say but it felt like a corner, the kind that might put a lot of people in another country.

"My name is Jim Rusk, and I was the leader of the True North," Jim began and he didn't stop. He told it all. What they'd done, and when and to whom. Rhan felt a tingle crawling over his skin. There was no way back from this. Some roads you couldn't travel twice.

Jim already had the papers out of his briefcase and he began to read out loud. Financial statements, Rhan realized. He listened to the numbers and he was staggered, not just by the golden flow, but where it had come from. Unimpeachable corporations, high-profile private donations, sterling companies that often stood hand in hand with different levels of government. And as Rhan listened he could hear something else, check books shutting, doors slamming, a wild scrambling to turn off the taps and wipe up the smallest drops left on the ground. In half an hour Jim Rusk dried up an entire river of money and opened canyons between people who'd been confederates. He cut off the lifeline to them, and to himself. The True North would starve to death, and that would be only the beginning. The legal battle was going to be ugly and long. With a pang Rhan realized this brave man might not see the end of it. Retribution from the phantom cells would probably be swift. If he went to jail, it might keep him alive.

When he was finished, Rusk gathered his papers up carefully, no longer just records but evidence.

"I know you'll make sure this gets the widest audience," he said and smiled wanly. "I'd go to the RCMP but I'm sure they'll come to me."

Rhan seized his hand and shook it. "Lee thought the world of you," he said.

He watched Jim Rusk walk away, thinking about the monk in his vision. Maybe it hadn't meant a holy man, but someone capable of devotion and sacrifice. It still wasn't a small thing.

Mark was already dubbing a copy from the master tape. He put them both in Rhan's hands.

"This is a life," Mark said, meeting Rhan's eyes, being certain he understood. "You can't put a price on it, but you're going to have to. Just make sure..."

"They treat it with respect," Rhan said.

The instructor nodded, then hesitated. "You're going to have an exciting career," he said, but it was a warning. "Not everyone's going to be happy about that. You're going to need a tough skin."

The words caught Rhan at an odd angle. He was nineteen years old and he'd buried both of his parents and his grandmother. He'd met only one of his own kind and he was gone now, too. He'd been alone most of his life.

"I've got skin like armor," Rhan said, and he felt the words ring inside him because they were true. "I don't think there's anything they could do to me."

Mark gave his shoulder a friendly push, setting him in motion. "Good man. Try to remember that. You might have to put it on your wall."

As Rhan dialed Willie Shine from Mark's office, he thought he heard a sound, distant and dreamlike, a woman screaming in rage.

◆

Thursday night Rhan dreamed of Chelsey, the golden Labrador retriever that had once belonged to Lee. In his dream she didn't belong to anybody, she was just running through an open field on a beautiful day, her golden coat shining in the sun, not going anywhere but running the way only animals can, in complete abandon and joy. He saw her from a distance and he didn't call her. It was enough just to watch her, the unchained freedom that took his breath away.

"I love doing special effects. It's one of the perks."

Rhan sat up in bed, suddenly awake, darkness all around him. He didn't just hear that, he'd felt it. But where was he?

"Close your eyes."

Rhan hesitated, then lay back down. He shut his eyes and he saw him, the Iceman, but like he'd never seen a human being. He wasn't that ghost on the field, translucent and scared. He was white and gold at the same time—impossible but he was!—as if light was coming out of his skin, every cell glowing with well-being. And his face—he was enjoying Rhan's amazement, loving the astonishment, as if he had spent his whole life planning this surprise.

"Are you all right?" Rhan said, not out loud but in his mind.

Lee laughed. Rhan could feel the gust of delight in his own body.

"Oh, you could say that. We're all...pretty all right."

"We?" Rhan said.

Lee seemed to step aside and Rhan saw a silhouette, a brilliant outline, not ethereal and distant but solid and real, real enough for a bingo shirt. Rhan felt a burst of gratitude in his chest and hot water behind his tightly shut eyelids.

Gran didn't speak—she didn't have to. Rhan just knew that what he was feeling now, the joy, the completion, the reunion, was a gift she had been given, too, with her own child. No one was wasted! Rhan thought. No one was lost.

"Tough old lady," Lee teased. *"I can hardly get into trouble. But, listen—thanks."* There was no sense of space but he seemed to draw closer, pull in for a secret. *"Two presents."* He held up one finger. *"It won't happen for years yet, but—"* He hesitated, enjoying the dramatic effect. *"It's a girl."*

A girl? Rhan wondered. A *baby* girl?! But Lee was already holding up another finger.

"Second present— it's all real."

Rhan felt the gift blow through him like a wind, larger and greater than he could hold at one time, a thought that blew all the doors open.

And Lee loved that, too. He was grinning, pure elf. *"See you,"* he said, and it was all gone.

"See you!" Rhan blurted out loud, sorry but grateful, the experience still echoing in him.

Beside him in the dark, Jen stirred.

Her back was to him and he pulled her in tightly. He was there, he realized. He had all that he needed—the sword, the armor, a kingdom and a princess, a real one. He was that knight and he had more than one foot in the Magic Nation. Way more. He kissed her shoulder and nestled his face in close against her.

"I'm having a wonderful dream," Jen murmured.

"Me, too," Rhan whispered into her hair.

ACKNOWLEDGMENTS

The Cinema, Television, Stage and Radio program taught at the Southern Alberta Institute of Technology was one of the most important corners of my life. I have the highest regard for the professionals who teach there and I wish to thank them on two counts: for sparking a love of writing that has never dimmed and for generously sharing their work and insight when I returned to research this book.

Although the CTSR program is real, I have tampered with circumstance to create a work of fiction. For an accurate profile of this exciting and demanding course contact the Southern Alberta Institute of Technology, 1301 16th Avenue N.W., Calgary, Alberta, Canada, T2M 0L4.

Also, I wish to thank Wm. Plaetinck, Head of the Tec Voc Broadcasting Department in Winnipeg, Manitoba, for giving so freely of his time and expertise. He welcomed me into his classroom and patiently answered my questions month after month. If there are errors of technology in this book, they are mine alone.

Diana Wieler
1997

To enjoy the whole RanVan trilogy,
read
RanVan: The Defender
and
RanVan: A Worthy Opponent